CLACKAMAS LITERARY REVIEW

2009, Volume XIII
Clackamas Community College, Oregon City, Oregon

CLR
CLACKAMAS LITERARY REVIEW

Editor in Chief

Ryan Davis

Assistant Editors

Monique Babin
Corey Donaghue
Betty Esterberg
Janet Hensley
Angela Hughes
Lauren Ogden
Tobias Peterson
Andrew Shepherd
Mary Stepec
Jill Stukenberg
Mary Wysong-Haeri

Cover Art

Angela Hughes

Cover Design

Kirstin van Dyke

The Clackamas Literary Review is published annually at Clackamas
Community College. Manuscripts are read from September 1st to January
31st and will not be returned. By submitting your work to CLR, you
indicate your consent for us to publish that work in our print journal and
on our website. This issue is $10; back issues are $5. Clackamas Literary
Review, 19600 Molalla Avenue, Oregon City, Oregon 97045.
ISBN 978-0-615-41497-3. Printed by Lightning Source.

http://www.clackamasliteraryreview.org

Contents

Editor in Chief's
Note

Fiction

Poetry

Essay

Editor in Chief's Note

I have always been fascinated by trains and railroads. My grandfather spent many years working for the Union Pacific, at the Albina Yard, in Portland, Oregon, and he was my railroading inspiration. Some of my earliest memories are of the two of us playing with a battery powered train, spending what seemed like hours watching it spin round an oval of tin tracks, blowing real smoke from its stack as it flew into a homemade tunnel. The smoke would collect in the tunnel and be drug through by the pull of the engine, exiting in one big plume. The writing you'll read in this issue is just like this—you'll see it coming, but the words arrive in one big burst, enveloping you in all their power. This connection is easy to make because some of the authors you will read write about trains, so I know mine is not a limited fascination.

During a recent presentation on railroads by the Canby (OR) Historical Society, I learned that in the early part of the 20th century, the railroads were so well-run that passengers could cross the country and often arrive within 30 minutes of their scheduled arrival time. This was an amazing feat, given all the difficulties this growing form of transportation had to face. I wish that, like the trains, this issue of CLR arrived closer to schedule, but it has finally reached the station. I would like to thank the authors for their enduring patience, the assistant editors for all their help, and you, for reading what I know is an issue filled with wonderful writing.

Ryan Davis

Birthright
Danielle Bauman

1.
My mother used to love New Year's Eve.
She wore sequined dresses and drank scotch,
like a man, she would say.
Even when it wasn't a holiday she would indulge.
She'd fight me off like some rodent,
screaming and stumbling to the shower to cry,
till a sound sleep took her.
I comforted myself by believing she was sleeping beauty,
kissing her in hopes that she'd wake up.
In the morning she asked if I still loved her, and I did.
Then the door started going unlocked,
and we would get robbed.
First the VCR, then the T.V., then we were asked to leave.
We moved from the trendy Park Slope brownstones,
glory days gone;
my mother found a sponsor and a safe addiction to caffeine.

2.
The first time I encountered marijuana it smelled like burnt
toothpaste.
My father smoked in the bathroom, letting the shower run
so the scent could rise with steam to thicken.

I sat on my parents bed
drawing in the scent,
a mysterious cologne I was not allowed to watch him apply.
My ruby slippers clicked.
I was proud in my position:
his dinner and a movie date,
companion during Sunday chores.
On Christmas Eve,
while Catholic families
trudged off to midnight mass,
we sat on barstools.
I made friends with the regulars
sneaking sips from my father's drink;
there's no place like home.

3.
After my mother stopped drinking,
she had visions of Jesus walking with his flock
through our hallway—
proof that she would be alright.
In the darkness,
I saw my inheritance spread out before me,
every indulgence marked with yellow caution tape.
I would learn to relish in the florescence of sobriety,
the only way to rebel against overgrown children.

4.
But someday I will creep in, turn the shower to full blast,
and pour a drink of my mother's Johnnie Walker.
I'll roll joints from my father's Altoid box,
and leave messages in the steam.

Self-portrait with Woodstove

Loren Graham

Bright flashes are the days, dark are the nights.
The snow descends, rises, shrinks, and decays.
Above, icicles accrue and decline.
A whole cord of locust slowly goes away.

The house expands and contracts, pops and knocks.
On his glasses, prints and specks appear.
He sits by the stove in the same chair, eyes locked.
Fresh silver materializes in his hair.

His life gets shorter. A day. Another day.
He feels it, but is numb, like something flayed.

Who is this man? He wishes he could know.
He wishes he could hear the *beneath* of things,
the way the owl can hear, beneath the snow,
the vole in its most surreptitious scratchings.

Hunger

Rick Henry

She in a thin summer dress, shivering in the heat. He sweating, seated, squinting at the paper on the table. She removing pots, pans from the pantry. He sweating, squinting at the paper on the table. She testing each pot against tomorrow's dinner, Wednesday's dinner, Saturday's dinner. He sweating, squinting at the letters on the paper. She measuring each pan from the pantry against the future. He swearing at the letters blurred with sweat. She separating keeps from sells. He swearing at the pen that slips through the sweat in his fingers. She separating the sells from the hocks. He dropping the pen to the table. She thinking about the egg in the ice box. He running his hands through his hair, running his sweat through his fingers. She thinking about the grocer and bills. He reading between the lines to the pots and pans in the keeps and hocks. She thinking about holes. He reading between the lines to the thin summer dress. She thinking about letters on the paper. He reading between the lines to Wednesday's bills. She thinking about the ink that runs and mixes with sweat and stains the table. He reading between the lines to Saturday's bills. She thinking about the indelible. He reading between the lines to the inevitable. She thinking about the note on the floor. He reading between the lines to the egg in the ice box. She thinking about life in the margins. He reading the margins for signs of life. She measuring a life. He reading the writing on the wall. She measuring the water in the pan. He hearing the sound of footsteps. She measuring the steps on the stairs. He hearing the note on the door. She feeling the pins in her hair. He feeling the hole in his stomach. She hearing the soft inhale. He bracing himself and picking up the pen and sweating over the margins and forgetting between the lines and thinking to the next meal and the pots and the pans and the egg in the ice box and the hole in her stomach and signs.

Les Hommes

Rick Henry

A vast emptiness in a small room. A large pile of dirt. A helmet rises, peeking from the peak. Just a peek. Just a touch. The helmet sinks out of sight. Eternal emptiness. No writing on the walls. No music in the air. No crickets, no birds. Two helmets rise, peeking from the pile. From the hole in the dirt. They slowly sink out of sight. No diversions in the emptiness. No kisses. No murmurs, sweet nothings, whispered wooings. Two helmets rise, cautiously, eyes exposed under the metal, nostrils fluted, mouths grimaced. Two helmets sink slowly out of sight. No sound in the silence. Deadly silence. Not even grunts and the one, two, three, and heave from the hole in the pile of dirt in the middle of the small room. There's no room to move. No room for sounds, for the one, two, three, and heave as a body appears, hands on feet, hands on hands, swung up and over the edge of the pile. Helmets rise, slowly, peeking at the body as it rolls over and over the dirt. Arms and legs akimbo. Helmets sink, slowly, hair on end, perpetually on end in the endless eternity. Silent eternity without the sounds of sweet nothings, without the hopes of sweet nuzzlings, without the smell of spring. Silent grunts. Hands on feet. Hands on hands. Helmet on the rise. A body, up, over the edge and down, arms and legs kimboed.

Grimaces sinking. Hearts sinking. Helmets sinking. Endless winter. Eternal chill. Helmets rise. Frozen breath over the top of the pile. Stale air. Miasmic and deadly air. Helmets sink. Hands on feet. Hands on hands. Bodies rise. Bodies tumble. Helmets rise. Helmets sink. Arms and legs, uniformed and uninformed. An array of thighs and knees and calves all poised, softly angled, softly splayed as if in wanton disarray ... as if in wanton disarray.

There's Another Blue

Mark Liebenow

The necrotized blue
      of bloated bodies grappled by hooks
      from summer vacation lakes.

Ashen blue
      that fuses
      a dead wife's lips.

Pewter blue
      of baby's skin
      born without breath.

Comet blue that scours sour hope
      off steps descending
      into despair.

This is not lapis lazuli blue
that sent a thousand ships
in search of art.
Virgin Mary's pure blue
that showers hope
over downtrodden poor.
The blue coalesced by some
young, cathartic event.
Blue of deep, iridescent shimmer.

8

The moody Miles Davis' blues,
or faded blue
of mother's dear old dress.
But chipped lead blue
       of abandoned windowsills
       blistering in sun.

Sad translucent blue
       glazing the empty rim
       of Bombay dry gin.

Silverfish blue
       trudging home every day
       to empty shadow rooms.

It's not the color of your death
I mind, but the color of air
when even this of you is gone.

Dreamer
Arthur Gottlieb

At the seawall
where signs say
Swim at your own risk,
tides rise,
wave you away.

Masts,
riding at anchor
in the harbor,
point past stars
running rings
around Saturn,
parked docilely
at the dock, waiting
for the owner
to take it for a spin.

He knows the globe
is more then an old theater,
in which you play chess
with a checkered past.

It can be plastic,
twirled at the tip
of a credit company's card.

Uncanny as it seems, I'm
no Atlas, but my fingers
have walked miles of maps
in the yellowing pages
of ancient Geographics.

I've come to measure
heavens by the heaviness
of having both feet
on the ground, calculating

the distance from death
by the pull of gravity,
while reaching for moons.

Rising

Laurie Frankel

Camille was Jewish, had Jewish hair and was therefore suicidal. Unexpectedly encountering her reflection in the Macy's storefront window was an arresting experience. Her hair, wet and tame upon leaving the house, appeared dry, large and expanding—her own private Big Bang. No matter how she was feeling, upon seeing the poof, taking off as if a gun had been fired, all confidence evaporated. Her mood reverted to the level with which she was comfortable: general and undistinguished misery.

You would think something as inanimate, dead really, as hair would not be prone to hi-jinx and unanticipated relocation but such was the nature of kink. Camille reached into her briefcase for a covered rubber band to subdue her ever-expanding universe into a tight bun, and while the aftermath of brute force is never pretty, she was, for the time being, assured her hair would be where she last left it.

Occasionally fueled by the life force of delusion, Camille engaged in costly salon visits and the latest in designer product[1]. The result: a miracle of Lourdes for

---

[1] Ouidad Climate Control, Zero Frizz Anti Frizz, Cowboy Magic Detangler & Shine, MOP Defining Cream, Garnier Nutrisse Ultra Doux Shampoo & Conditioner, Frederic Fekkai Luscious Curls, Bumble & Bumble Brilliantine, Enjoy Straightener, Yanai Van Curl Lift, Aveda Be Curly Curl Control, Curl Friends Seduce Pomade, One'n Only Frizz Remover, Tigi Bed Head Uptight Curl Maker, Clairol 3-in-1 Moisturizing Mousse, Curly Hair Solutions Curl Keeper, Unite 7 Seconds Leave-in Conditioner, Izzazu Super Scrunch, Paul Mitchell Gloss Drops Frizz-Free Defining Polish, Phytodefrisant Balm, Joico Ice Sculpting Lotion,

approximately forty-five minutes followed by a reversion to social blight.

Plenty of people, uglier, without complete sets of teeth managed the cycle of birth to death without intervention. Camille, however, systematically contemplated her own undoing over the years in chart format:

ACTIVITY	PRO	CON
Pills	In enough quantity, almost anything will do.	Panic, call 911 and they don't come fast enough. Get drunk first?
Hanging	Strong, visual impact.	Seems technical, lots of room for error.
Gun	Definitive (if don't chicken out).	Messy. Might not work, leave you maimed.
"Accident," ie bus	Quick, fast.	Unnecessarily involves others. Possibility of maiming or dismemberment.
Carbon Monoxide Poisoning	Knocked out.	Lots of prep, especially if you don't want to hurt someone else.
Anorexia	Can't think of any.	Slow road. Big commitment. Easy to intervene.

One bad day, shortly after a particularly painful breakup Camille found herself in the bathroom and, without

---

Redken All Soft Heavy Cream, Fantasia Frizz Buster Serum, Klorane Nourishing and Untangling Conditioning Balm, Graham Webb Head Games Moisturizing Bliss Shampoo, Matrix Liquid Shine, Sebastian Shaper Zero G, Salon Selectives Stay Flexible Finishing Spray, Kerastase Nutritive Elasto Curl Definition Forming Cream, Ouidad Botanical Boost.

direct intention, swept eight Ambien off the counter and tossed them into her mouth. She stuck out her tongue and looked at its reflection in the mirror. Eight pills sat like trailers after a storm on an aerial map only, with the saliva, they were starting to spread a bit like houses on shifting sand. She imagined living in the third pill from the left with a dog and a VW Bug. After several moments the tip of her tongue got cold and dry creating the urge to swallow. She scraped her tongue against her front teeth. The pills fell onto the ceramic basin clinking in twos and threes.

In between feeling depressed and wanting to kill herself Camille dated. She thought of initial meetings with strange men as auditions for skits or one-scene shorts—if you couldn't get a call back you weren't acting hard enough. Camille's first-date goal was not so much to gauge her own interest as to generate goodwill, be entertaining and make the cut. Her success rate was at the upper end of the bell curve, but, often, by date three Camille uncovered egregious fault (college dropout, Greenpeace vegan, multiple cat owner), lost interest and disappeared.

Bored and disgusted Camille went out one night and, under the influence of a long-island iced tea and a revolving disco ball, met Derek at *Tiny Bigs*. "Heaven must be missing an angel," Derek said.

"Why? Did you shoot one down?" Camille asked her voice muffled as her lips remained locked around the straw.

"No, but I'm going to," he said poking his index finger into her side.

"Don't touch," she said pulling away, still sipping.

"Let's dance." He held out his hand. Camille looked at Derek. His face was flawed, roman nose and deep forehead offset by full lips and a square jaw—handsome in a way she could handle.

"I'll buy you another," Derek said and separated Camille from her drink. He led her confidently through the crowd and danced with just enough rhythm to not embarrass and still be hetero. By night's end, she left him with the taste of her drink in his mouth and her number penned on the palm of his hand.

Camille prepared for their first official date the night before. After years of trial and error she learned her hair, like pizza, was better the next day. And, so, before bed, she shampooed, conditioned, damp dried and scrunched. She added a leave-in, a curl enhancer, relaxer and something for shine. She finger curled and blew her hair damp-dry with a diffuser, added duck bill clips for height and sat under the ionic bonnet hair dryer for twenty minutes then brushed her teeth and went to bed. Nineteen hours later she sprayed a light mist of booster and sat with her eyes closed at the kitchen table. Derek rang at 7:10p.

"I thought we'd drive into the city," he said as they walked out to his car. "I know a great restaurant on the water. Killer iced teas." He squeezed her arm and guided her down the walk.

Camille stopped. "Is that your car?" she asked.

"My baby," Derek said walking to the passenger side and unlocking the door of his fully-restored, '68 corvette convertible, red.

"Oh, nice, uh huh," Camille said searching her purse, belt loop and coat pockets for a hair clip. She checked her back pocket, front pockets and zippered section of her purse, twice. Her efforts were rewarded with a lint-covered piece of Dentyne, a licked stamp and a jumbo paper clip.

As they drove away a light breeze lifted and lowered segments of carefully constructed curls. Camille caught her reflection in the side view mirror: a fine layer of hair lifted then separated. Like bad-seed children, they soon headed in various directions.

Her palms grew moist and her mouth dry as she emptied the entire contents of her purse into her lap. "Forget

15

something?" Derek asked.

"No, I'm fine, I…" Camille said digging through the pile.

"Need to turn back?"

"No, everything's fine," she said holding the bent paper clip between her teeth as she reassembled her purse. When she was done she looked out the window, carefully patting the top of her head.

Three surface streets and two stoplights later they entered the onramp to the highway. Derek slipped in a CD of Vivaldi and winked. "Buckle up," he said and drove the stick into fourth then fifth gear. Camille's head snapped back. Her hair lifted like a rocket separating from its launch pad. As their speed increased the force of wind decimated all chemical bonds. One and a half miles later liftoff was complete.

Upon arrival at the restaurant, Camille corralled the mushroom cloud into a tight bun and stabbed it with the straightened paper clip. Derek opened her door and, as she took his outstretched hand, her hair unwound until it caught against the make shift straight pin. It came to rest low at the side of her neck like a goiter or a large fruit bat.

"You look lovely," Derek whispered and kissed Camille on the cheek. She lowered her eyes and gently touched the mass resting on her shoulder. They walked into the restaurant where Camille proceeded to drink in direct proportion to the growth against her neck. She blacked out on the ride home and woke at 3:00am to the sound of Derek snoring on the couch.

Date two did not involve natural forces or alcohol. At Derek's suggestion, they saw the movie, *High Fidelity*. Camille fell in love with Rob, the John Cusack character and wondered, as they exited the movie theater, if she should be dating him instead of Derek. Afterwards, over coffee, she noted, for every five or so comments Derek made, one was slightly humorous or intriguing (1.5 if you counted his uncle's shark attack). Rob's hit rate was 2:1 and while, rationally, Camille knew Rob was fictional and scripted she still felt, on some primal level, it was a fair comparison.

Afterward, in the car, Camille consented to a short make-out session during which she closed her eyes and pretended she was kissing Rob, then Derek, then Rob concluding Rob was the better kisser. And because in a very small place in the back of her head she knew Derek was Rob was Derek, that movies were not real and she was, in some ways, majorly fucked up, she agreed to another date and said good night.

Since Camille had irrationally concluded Derek was not long-term date material she made sex her third-date mission. When he arrived to pick her up she ambushed him at the door with a tray of pomegranate martinis and heated baby quiches. They never made it to *Tampopo Grill*.

After the act, Derek tried to run his fingers through Camille's hair. "Ow!" she said, "That's a knot," and sat up leaning in as Derek tried to disengage. "Stop," Camille said leaning in further. "Stop. Please. Now, ok. Straighten," she said. "Straighten your fingers and spread them as in no one finger touching the other." Derek nodded. "Now, remove. Slowly." Derek did as he was told and the two separated. Camille sat back against the headboard, legs crossed, hiding herself beneath a pillow. They looked at each other. "You can pet it," Camille said. "That's about it." She pulled two thick strands of hair behind her head and, without mechanical aid, secured them in a half square at the back of her head.

Derek leaned forward to look. "Magic," he said, buried his face in her neck and breathed in deeply.

Having consistent sex and access to Derek's 80 GB iPod was fun. So was learning what he had on TiVo (*Planet Earth, WWF Friday Night Smackdown*), where he wanted to vacation (Amalfi Coast) and who he admired past and present (Leonardo Da Vinci, Dean Kamen). She liked how he smelled and made a note: *Drakkar Noir* should they still be seeing each other come Christmas.

Navigating desire, self-loathing and generalized anxiety made Camille feel queasy and alive. Every week she was surprised they'd made it through another until, before she knew it, they'd hit the four-month mark leaving her thrilled but exhausted.

On a two-lane road, headed north to camp one last time before the weather turned, Camille looked out the car window. The sun, out just a moment ago, had gone away. Clouds rolled in and began erasing the contrast of tree against sky. A few more miles and the landscape turned atonal, without edges—a pasture was a fence was a cow. Everything fading, one into the other. Camille looked from the side window through the windshield to the dashboard and over to Derek. As the first raindrop fell, she came to know, for reasons incomplete yet unquestionable, she could never be happy.

And so it was one evening after dinner Camille told Derek to go. She listened to the squeak of sneakers crossing linoleum and while she wanted to stop him no words came. After she heard the door close she walked into the living room and parted the curtain to watch him leave. As he disappeared down the block there was a sense of Derek moving away in fast motion, of herself receding and, as a result, the creation of a deep opening. The easiest thing was to simply step in.

Camille dropped the curtain and went to bed. She slept all the next day and a good deal of Sunday. On Monday, she called in sick. At noon, she got up and made herself a piece of toast. She did not call Derek not out of any conviction or on moral grounds but because the option was simply no longer available to her. Instead, she picked up a pen and wrote:

Derek, take whatever you want from my apartment, except for me, of course, because, by the time you read this, I'll be on the other side, a TV test pattern. Other side. We don't believe in that, do we? (this is a suicide note just so there isn't any confusion later on.)

She ripped the page out of her notebook and put it in the garbage. She tore out a second sheet and began again:

My Dearest Derek Camille wrote, then scratched this out and tore out a third sheet. *Dear Derek, the raccoon was on the porch again. I know you said not to, but I threw him an apple slice. He held it in his paws and while we looked at each other he ate. I told him I was sad, for you and for me (me mostly). He chewed a bit, then looked up and, with caveman eyes said, Go. I asked him twice and both times, Go.*

I love you, Camille
PS The car is at the Park 'n Ride, extra key in the hallway drawer.
PPS This is a suicide note just so there isn't any confusion later on.

Once Camille signed the note, her actions locked in like a train on a track. She prepared as if she had a routine appointment at a predetermined hour, preparing breakfast, doing dishes, brushing her teeth. She skipped makeup but not moisturizer, filed a nail but left on old polish, sprayed her hair and let it air dry. She did everything necessary to make herself comfortable on the drive over.

Camille dug her hands into her coat pockets and tucked her head against the wind as she walked toward the mid-span of the bridge. She felt as if she were walking to the dentist or the nail salon, an appointment set up by herself for the management of herself. One last to-do.

Her hair caught in the corners of her mouth and sunglass frame. Then a crosswind cut, whipping strands in the opposite direction. It burned. She tied her hair back into a tight bun and heard screams of protest. She turned. Two young children ran ahead of their parents. Camille was taken with the idea of the inanimate protesting and closed her eyes and held her hair as she listened to the high-pitched squeals.

She opened her eyes and leaned against the rail and looked down to see the wind lifting finger-like waves and dropping them, then, out further, she saw Alcatraz, alone, pointy and sharp, and beyond that Treasure Island.

Without direct contemplation Camille found herself on top of the guardrail thinking of treasure, pirates, traitors then *Trader Joe*. Instantly, *We Cut Out the Middleman* from a store placard came into her mind as she stood atop the outside girder, her back against the rail. She focused on the idea of the middleman and cutting him out till it made perfect sense to jump as a means of going direct and then she did.

As she left the bridge, the brilliance of *Trader Joe* pained her as things of intense beauty do, but she found she wasn't so much moving toward the island as it was the island getting taller, rising up. Everything seemed to be moving but her, as if she were already drowning, in the sky. She never felt herself falling so much as it seemed to be the clouds rising, like a curtain against the blue. Then the bridge ascending, its concrete supports thrusting up through the air and the water following, pushing toward. Her face was distorted by the natural forces, skin draping like fabric over an armature of bone, but it was never Camille falling, never that, until after two hundred and fifty feet, she hit. Complete, blank and black.

Day turned to night as the sea rose twenty, thirty, then forty feet above her where she hung enveloped by the universe. Her hair, tamed by the water, waved around her head—an animated crown of glory. She felt enormous and lovely, the desire to breathe magnificent. And then, the whole process reversed. Stories of water pulled past and down, a thickening dark thinned to light and the pressure receded till she met the surface, her stage revealed, and bobbed to the waterline with only one shoe. She inhaled and coughed. Blood ran from her nose. A rescue worker pulled her from the water unscathed except for her shoulder, improperly angled, and broken capillaries on her cheeks and chin.

   Wrapped tight in a blanket and seated, Camille braced against the wind as she and the crew sped across the bay. While she knew she was seated (she could measure her placement against those in the boat) the sensation of rising continued. She seemed to hover slightly. A cloud cluster passed and the sun flashed off the boat's chrome safety bar. Camille shielded her eyes. When she opened them she saw herself reflected back—her dark hair, wet and heavy, dancing away from her as they motored to shore.

The Painter of Horror Tries His Hand at Tranquility

Ann Linde

He has to leave the faces blank. Four girls on a bridge, known by their different-colored hair. It's horrible that one is turning to us. It's horrible that the others are looking at the water, judging its depth, how far they'd have to fling themselves. Or they'll push her over. The trees are complicit. There are dwelling places but not a village. The sky has succumbed before the girls; the sun is only a reflection. He hasn't given her a mouth.

We Couldn't Keep Him Anymore

Ann Linde

We couldn't keep him anymore, so we put Jesse on a bus, sand in his eyes and hair, and bought bubblegum in his honor. None of us knew where the bus stopped, but it was sure to be a town with a diner. A muscular middle-aged waitress would surely take a liking to Jesse and give him a home. They'd have a dog, a pit bull maybe, tied with rope to the patch of grass in their yard. Jesse would put wheels on the Chevy and get it started up in the mornings. When the circus came to town they'd go. They'd play spades and hold drinking contests between the two of them and one day Jesse would win. The rest of his life would shine like grease on the griddle and she would call him Hotcakes.

Good Luck

Ann Linde

Hubby drums his knees, rattles
in our tin can.

The Boss shakes a good-luck
charm before he oils
his boar bristles and
pastes up another

randy-cap comic.
Hubby makes egg yolks

appear in his
out-of-work arms.
Lady, who's paying—
how do you fare?

Hubby and his beer trade
silver cap-toothed grins.

Inside my red-and-white dress
I buzz like the Frigidaire.
I'll step out of here
so cool, when

I kiss off
my lips will freeze to the metal.

Blinking Lights

William Archila

At a crossing gate, I hear the whistle
then the rumble, wheels popping and grinding

shaking the bed of gravel, the pile of dirt
holding up the roadway. Suddenly, clank and roar,

one hundred tons of iron
race down the line like a long

black river rushing through the city,
a shot of smoke cutting the sky.

I remember the plug run I rode as a boy
with the windows down, wind swollen with rain,

hills stepping aside. My grandmother in a flower dress
sat beside me, no apron, no basket full of hens.

She brought coffee, French bread stuffed
with beans, cream and avocado. We watched

tin huts and their trail of smoke,
stray dogs rambling along the rails,

country girls, clay pitchers, baskets of fruit
perched on their heads. Here, for the first time

I see how they live in the mountains,
running across coffee fields, scurrying like ants

they crawl into the cracks of the earth
as the sun goes down, lurk in their shadow.

Everything's red up front in the cab, coals
with a core of glowing fire.

No sound comes from the engine driving on
beyond the green bay, stacked

logs chained to its flat beds,
pushing into the failing light.

I gaze at a shack - broken roof, jagged
holes. A shirtless man

stands in the doorway getting smaller,
smaller as the train pulls away.

In the Pit

William Archila

There's Concha selling gum and cigarettes,
bunching her lips like a coin purse to kiss me,
always in sandals, ankles scratched. If you talk to her
her voice carries the sound of grass chewed by cows.

See the man sitting on the gutter, coffee can
between his feet, he was a carpenter
until they broke him down with electricity,
psychology, then photographed
him uncombed, staring.

Atop the cliff, tin huts choking on coils of smoke
where dust buries itself beneath the tongue,
the shallow of graves breathe in the sun.

Those are the buzzards holding meetings way up
over our heads, spiraling with wings spread wide.
And the copper children, dressed in rags, ashy knees
staring at us, they shine shoes,
military shoes, shoes of bodyguards, those who drink
the slime off the street. They cart packages,
they are under priced, under ten,
                        the children I mean.

This is the slum we are walking in
where the country inhales, gasps for air,
raises its asphalt to the light
                                    as if letting out
a circle of nothingness, a hole in the broken ground.

Balancing Between the Trains

Harding Stedler

Parallel rails
divide the mining camp,
and the world passes through
on steel.
In dimly lighted passenger cars,
wealthy merchants steal
our poverty from the night.
Our curtains wave
through open windows
as we sleep among the whistles,
our only way to welcome strangers.

In daylight, between afternoon trains,
we learn to balance
on the tracks
and gather spilled coal in buckets
for the night fires.
The new-coal smell
keeps strangers at bay.
The burned-coal clouds
hem guardian hillsides
that frame the sooted shacks.

Our world is lonely,
and we are trapped
in a valley of despair.
At the company store,
we smile without teeth
and pose for disposable cameras.

From The Darkness Right
Under Our Feet

Patrick Michael Finn

One or two sewer rats would scatter down the stairs whenever I opened the basement door. They were bigger than bricks and moved like blunt lengths of gray pipe on four legs, whipping their cable-thick tails as they jumped the last step and ran off into the darkness right under our feet. We kept the dogfood at the top of the stairs, and that's what the rats were after.

The first night I saw them, I stumbled back into the kitchen and yelled out, "There's rats on the stairs!"

"Aw, Jesus Christ Crowned," my father mumbled from the next room, sprawled like a sick bear on the couch in front of the television, shirt open, pants undone, scratching the hairs on his gut. "We don't have any rats in this house."

In the horror movies, rats stand on their hind legs, and maybe you'll see them nibbling something in their claws while they eye the terrified people they've snuck up on with a black glare of malice. The rats in our house had no such theatrical grace. When the lights hit them, they ran, clobbered down the basement stairs. You knew where they were going, and you knew they would stay. And you knew they would come up from the basement and get into all the places there were to get. The cabinets, the drawers, the dog food. Rats meant filth, and the shame of filth too. They'd bite you, sure. Rats, I knew for a fact, could squeeze through a surprisingly small slice of space given their girth, under doors, vent slats. Their bones could bend and fold like rubber under all that gray meat.

I begged my parents to call an exterminator, buy some rat poison, anything.

"You probably saw a mouse," my mother said. "A little harmless baby mouse."

I wanted to send Glory down after them, but my father wouldn't let him in the house. Glory was kept in the garage to protect the mower and tools, even when it got so cold that the gas in my father's truck froze. Once I tried to sneak Glory down anyway after my parents went to bed. I thought he'd find the rats and eat them. But he didn't even make the basement stairs. As soon as he hit the kitchen he went nuts and tore through the whole house. He barked and growled and knocked things over. Then he puked all over the couch. By then my parents were awake, and my father stabbed his finger into my chest over and over for that night's many catastrophes: bringing Glory into the house, two broken lamps, the vomit on the furniture, and What the hell would have happened if someone had broken into the garage and taken all the goddamn tools?

It was almost Thanksgiving and the rats were getting more brazen. I found one right in the dog food when I opened the bag. I yelped and fell back into the kitchen, but the rat just crawled out and bolted down the stairs before my parents saw him.

Why couldn't I just move the dog food out to garage?

"Because," my father told me, "Glory'll eat it all. Don't ask me again."

I even showed my parents the articles from the Joliet paper about how bad the rat problem had gotten ever since the storm sewer restoration. The rats were coming up through toilets. Health officials encouraged citizens to keep their toilet seats down and weighted with cinder blocks when they weren't using them. And when you had to use the toilet, you flushed twice before you sat so that the rats wouldn't squeeze through and bite you on your ass. I didn't dare sit down on the toilet. I held it all in until my insides folded and ached and bubbled on the verge of colonic rupture. I was actually hunched over and holding my stomach when I pointed out another newspaper article to my father, but he just moaned and said, "Oh, goddamnit, enough about the rats. They only get rats in niggerville. We're clean people."

I decided trying to sneak Glory into the basement again. I planned on finding some rats and hitting one over the head with a wrench and sticking it in a garbage bag to show my parents. My father had many wrenches, and I took one and hid it in one of my bedroom drawers. The only way I could do it, find and kill a rat, was to have Glory down there with me. I'd have to bring him in on a leash to keep him from going wild and barfing all over the house. The plan seemed impossible. Glory didn't even have a real leash. I had to make one out of a belt and some rope. Impossible or not, I had to go through with it. I'd found two more rats in the dog food. This time I didn't fall or yell. I slammed the basement door so hard the floors and windows throbbed. My father marched into the kitchen and asked me what the hell my problem was. Halfway through my answer, my mother ran in and my father shook his head and said, "He's a chickenshit is what. Scared of his own farts."

Then, just when I needed him the most, Glory got sick. His hair started falling out in raw patches, and he squirted diarrhea all over the garage. He stopped eating and just drank water and lanked around on the cold garage floor. I found him dead one morning when I went out to feed him. He didn't jerk or move at all when I opened the door. He lay there and I knew he was dead. This was near Christmas on the last day of class before vacation. But I said his name anyway. I said, "Hey, Glory."

34

I cried and my father asked me if I wanted to stay home from school. I didn't. I had something to prove, riding red-eyed on the bus in the cold, the kids I went to school with asking what was wrong, then saying, "Oh, shit. Sorry, man," when I told them.

That night I took the wrench and the garbage bag down to the basement by myself. I turned on the one dull bulb that hung from a wire and saw a rat skitter along the wall to the dark by the crawlspace. I dropped the wrench and it went *clang* on the concrete floor my father had painted "wine." The basement walls and stairs were painted "wine" too. Every year he planned to fix the basement up, and every year the only things down there were some boxes, a freezer for a few dead Michigan fish pulled from a dinky campground pond the summer before, the crawlspace, and now rats. All his talk about a pool table and carpeting and a bar. He said the guests would like the color "wine."

This house just sucks *big dicks*, I said.

This first night of Christmas vacation was always supposed to be the biggest glowing thrill, no matter how bad the freeze was blowing outside. But Glory was dead and his food was already gone, making the rats hungrier, crazy, so hungry they'd squeeze under the basement door and crawl into my bed to gnaw my fingers and eyes. While my parents sat safe and warm upstairs, not believing me, watching their stupid funny programs on the television. And fat. They were both so fat and lazy, ambling into the kitchen during ads in lumpy steps that shook the floors to snack on crackers and Christmas cookies.

"Wine."

I hadn't picked up the wrench, since my eyes were pursed, then wide and scared, flinching to catch whatever it was I thought was moving right outside the range of my sight at each corner, and I was too stiff to drop for the two seconds it would take to just bend over and grab it.

35

My father went into the kitchen, *lump lump lump lump lump*, and stopped at the cabinets. Cracker box plastic crackled, and the refrigerator door was opened for the gallon of whole milk he would drink straight from the bottle to wash down the crackers. And the cookies. Then my mother went into the kitchen, but her lumps were muffled. She wore slippers around the house, so she went *lumph lumph lumph lumph* when she moved around. My father was always barefoot.

Well hell then, I thought, I'm not fat and lazy like you up there. Goddamn both of you. I was so not fat and so not lazy that I seethed and surged red and, clutching the black trash bag, marched straight back to the darkest part of the basement. I hoisted myself into the crawlspace, flat on my back in the sand under the short ceiling lined with pipes and spiderwebs. I immediately discovered a pair of rats. They were huge, and they were screwing. Together, mounted, they moved a few inches away. I panicked, forgot that I was in the crawlspace and slammed my head into the pipes above. The scream I let out was a brokenly hoarse pubescent rasp. Then one of the rats squealed, and in an immeasurable blur or motion I managed to kick crawlspace sand into my eyes, tangle myself in the garbage bag, swing the wrench left, right, which struck the pipes and plugged me right back just as fast. First on my cheek, then *bang*, my nose. My whole skull rang with a thrum of dazzling pain. I choked up nose blood that gushed down my throat.

I finally spilled out of the crawlspace and stumbled, bowlegged, back to the stairs. My cheekbone tingled. I almost touched it, but the numbness parted with a stunning ache that pulsed from the core of my brain. I had no captured rat, no wrench, no bag, no rat bites to show my parents so they could rush me to the emergency room.

And I was still bowlegged. I had crapped my pants.

And my parents were still snacking in the kitchen when I opened the door. My mother, stammering to ask, "What happened, what happened?" grabbed her coat to rush me to the hospital.

"No way," my father said. "We're not taking him to any goddamn hospital. The doctors'll think *we* did this. If he wants to knock the shit out of himself, let him. Let him go to bed and hurt until he hurts himself out of deciding to act like a beached feeb next time he gets an itch to throw himself down the stairs."

"Here, open up," he said, opening then probing my mouth with his fingers that tasted like newspaper. "No, he didn't lose any teeth, and no," he said to the ceiling as he took back his fingers and wiped them vigorously on his brown bathrobe, "he's not going to any hospital."

My mother stood behind him with her hands over her mouth.

Then he glared down at me where I stood, bleeding and bowlegged. His glare twisted into a sneer. "What in the *hell?*" he said. "Did you shit your pants?"

A cool nugget of dook ran down my leg and snuck out of a pant cuff. Right onto the bright waxed kitchen linoleum.

"You did! My God!" he said. "You messed your trousers. You soiled your goddamn panties like a goddamn babygirl."

He spun around and told my mother (as if she hadn't noticed the turd or her husband's disgrace) that I had actually dumped a pie in my shorts. At which point my mother sadly shook her head and quietly exited the kitchen.

"Get those off," my father said, and when I started to strip right there, he whined, "In the bathroom, in the bathroom. Get those clothes off and soak that mess off. Fill the tub, fill the tub! Get in that shower and now. Lord God,

37

only retards and faggots crap their shorts. Which one are you?"

I had pulled the curtain shut.

Which answer would have satisfied him?

Snow covered the streets the next day, but I was too dismal to enjoy it. Rats were waiting for me in every cabinet, drawer, shoe, pocket, and corner of the house. Were they even crouching over the doorways I might walk through, waiting to leap down and tear through the veins in my neck? I couldn't even look into the bowl of soup my mother made for lunch. The meat was rat meat. The onions had been licked in the night by some starving rat's wet, red tongue. I had to get out of the house.

I told my mother I was going to the library, but I actually took the bus to Washington Street, the main drag that cut through the part of town everybody called niggerville. I wanted to find some black kids my age and ask them about how they handled living with rats. They would know how to trap and kill them with cunning city resourcefulness. I stripped off the bandages on my cheek and nose on the way down so they would see that I was really just like them, another veteran of the rodent-wild streets.

I found some black kids having a snowball fight in the lot behind Joliet East High. They stopped playing when I approached.

"Excuse me," I said.

"Yeah?"

"Do you have rats in your houses?"

There were five or six of them. The tallest, oldest of them had on a Chicago Bears stocking cap, and I could tell he didn't at all like the question. "*What*?" he said.

"Rats," I told him. "I have rats in my house," I said. I pointed to the cuts on my face. "See? I got bit by rats."

Two of the youngest boys ran away yelling about how I had rabies. The oldest kid grabbed my coat and threw it way up into a tree. "Hey!" I said.

"Hey right," he answered.

They slapped me down, turned me over and pushed my face into the snow. When I lifted my eyes I saw two spots of nose blood in the icy white ground.

"Go put your rabies somewhere else," one of them said. They all walked away laughing. Then I couldn't reach my coat. It hung on a high branch, one arm slowly swinging in the cold breeze, waving me away from my terrible idea.

There was no way I was going to tell my parents that I had gone to niggerville, so I told them a bum had stolen my coat when I got up to use the library bathroom, and, because my father hated homeless people, he believed me.

"Don't ever leave your stuff with winos around," he said. "Those goddamn lazy animals'll take anything that isn't nailed down."

That night I heard a rat scratching the plaster down to dust in the wall right next to my bed. I pulled the covers over my head and waited for him to claw through. I couldn't stand it. I jumped out of bed and stood wide awake in the center of my room until dawn.

By this time I had long given up any hope for any help from either of my parents. Now they were too busy decking everything with tinsel and lights, cluttering the front yard with clunky lit-up plastic figures of Santa, his reindeer, the Holy Family, baking stacks of cookies I for once refused to eat, flooding the house with stereo carols by Crosby and Como, never noticing how I, their only son, had grown thinner and paler from lack of food and sleep, from constantly pacing the house wide-eyed and trembling, unable to sit *anywhere* from fear that a rat might crawl out from under a table, chair, or bed to gnaw and chew the tendons in my feet; never noticing how I, their only son, quit drinking water,

39

quit bathing in water, wouldn't touch water to brush my teeth or even rinse my hands, knowing the rats had invaded every pipe and waterway in, around, and beneath our house, wouldn't enter the bathroom but to quickly piss or, after flushing the toilet fifteen times, squat over the bowl with my pants around my shaking ankles to pass weak drippy gobs of yellow malnutrition.

Finally, on Christmas Eve, during Midnight Mass, right before Holy Communion, my reluctant hunger and wash strike got the best of me. I passed out during the Sign of Peace, collapsing into the next family just as they turned around to shake our hands.

In the car, my mother fanned my face with the parish holiday bulletin while my father hit the gas for home.

"Are you going to throw up?" he asked.

"No," I told him.

"You sure?"

"I'm sure."

I gave them one last chance. "Do you know why I fainted?" I asked in a pathetic rasp.

"No," my father said. "Why?"

"Because of the rats. I'm so scared of the rats I can't sleep, and I can't eat."

Nobody said a word for about a block. I could tell we were almost home, but not there yet. My father pulled over and stopped. He rested his head on the back of his seat, breathed a few times, then turned around and said, "You're driving yourself sick. And you're driving your mother and I crazy, if you want to know the whole truth."

My mother said my father's name and placed her hand on his arm. It's Christmas, she was saying in her own way, and our son is sick.

"Let me finish," he told her.

He ran his hand through his hair, then turned around again and said, "We just *do not* have rats in our house. Do you

understand me? We *do not* have rats. Now for the love of
Christ will you stop talking about it? We don't have rats. We
just don't."

I thought my mother would have stepped in again,
but she didn't. She just waved the bulletin at my face and
stared out the window until we got home.

On Christmas morning, when it was still dark, as I lay
in bed with my hands locked behind my head, listening to yet
another rat scratching through the wall, I decided I needed to
run away from home. I got up and crammed some clothes
into my backpack. Then I decided what I would do for work:
I would load up some of my father's tools and hitchhike from
city to city, fixing anything that was broken for a few bucks
under the table. In my mind the West was still a dry, ratless
region where I could finally settle in the warm safety of a new
life.

When I opened the garage door to get the tools, I
found my Christmas present: a new dog with a red bow
around his neck. There was a sign hooked to his collar that
said: *Merry Christmas, My Name Is Glory II.* An older, dumb-
looking pound mutt my father had probably gotten for free, a
backhanded gift that would have to stay locked in the garage
to protect *his* mower and tools. I lifted the garage door and
set Glory II free. He ran down the block, shook off his red
bow and sign, then kept running and never came back.

I collected two hammers, a wrench, some
screwdrivers, and three boxes of nails. I had to dump two
pairs of jeans in order to fit the tools into my backpack.
Then I went to the kitchen to see what I could swipe for road
food. A cold blue dawn was rising. As I went through the
cupboards, I started to feel dizzy and light, like I might pass
out again. I sat down at the kitchen table, gathered strength,
rubbed my eyes. In the center of the table was a platter
stacked with my mother's Christmas cookies: sweet wreaths,

sugared bells, buttered angels, little trees blanketed with frosted snow.

I unpacked my clothes and returned all but one of the tools to the garage. Then I went back to the kitchen and gathered two fistfuls of cookies and put them in a paper bag, took them to my room, and crushed them to crumbs with a hammer. Then I opened the basement door, walked to the bottom step, and started a trail of crumbs. I sprinkled the broken wreaths, bells, angels, and trees up every step, then past the door, through the kitchen, down the hallway, then into the bedroom where both of my parents were sleeping.

I ended the trail where their chests rose and fell under the big down comforter, then on their faces, and around their mouths, which they smacked in hungry discomfort. I went back to the kitchen, sat cross-legged on top of the table, and waited.

##

When I finally climbed off the kitchen table, I let my feet touch the floor without the dread of rodents squirming and growing beneath it. I straightened with the first certainty I had ever felt, and I went to bed.

First my mother screamed. Then my father bellowed a masculine howl that quickly shot right up to shrill, a sound he'd never made, a shamefully zany shriek far more feminine than my mother's.

Had that scream come from me, he probably would have said, Don't be such a goddamn pansy, sneering and furious at what a sick little faggot his only son was.

42

safety in numbers

Ann Tweedy

it feels safe to be many women
at once—confusing
but safe. alongside the lawyer, the poet,
alongside them both, the dreams
of park-ranging, running something--a laundromat
or that historic hotel in fort bidwell. always
there are escape routes, both real and imagined,
from whatever i'm doing at the moment.   even my
relationships
are diverse, multiple. if i tire of one me,
there's another, close at hand, to be or imagine.
true, nothing holds me very tightly
(except maybe poetry, who has my heart in its hand
no matter what i do). but for everything else
i'm like water perpetually in transition
from one form to another and then back again. and who
knows
if the imagined lives proceed in a parallel universe
or if i'll ever get to live them. or how i escaped

the dangerous balance of a seemingly static life–
like that of mary, the preacher's wife from selmer tennessee,
who shot and killed the preacher
as he lay in bed, having followed his orders
for nine years according to the wifely

43

subordination his last sermon
propounded–like wearing during sex
the patent leather platforms
and wig that dismayed the southern jury,
like covering her bruises with make-up and lying
about how she got them,
like hiding the preacher's suffocations
of their infant daughter to make her stop.

late that tuesday night, the pressure
of being stuck got to be too much, and she pointed
the gun and accidentally or on purpose
released bird shot into him. "i'm sorry" she said to his
"why?"
before packing up and driving
their three girls to an alabama beachtown.
later she'd say working part-time at the post office
had helped her gain the confidence
to know she didn't have to
take and take it like a mouse. if only mary the preacher's wife
could have met mary the post office worker
before desperation set in, the preacher's wife
might have huddled in the arms of the worker
and forged a careful way out.

For The Man On My Side Of
The Road
(1927—)

Janet Lyn

While sitting on a booster seat, I saw my mother
leave for the first time. I did not want to believe
she had a job outside of me,
so I sang my nightly lullaby.

He sat down, smiled, and I
began to cry.
But he took me to the park, set up a table
of chess. Next to the road he taught me.

And I won and lost and won
and won. With him, my tears began to clear.
I ran my hand down his cast.
It was rough, solid, and white--

he let me color it red and black.
And we never drove to the bank
nor to the store (like she and I) but fed bread,
instead, to the ducks each day.

When the *Long-neckers* chased me to him
I screamed, but they always retreated at his sight,
he kneeling to capture me

45

and I burying my eyes into his chest.
When we found a small bird
who did not fly, I asked to bring it home
but lost heart when it flew
from his VW bus. He told me *It belongs*

in a tree—even with the hawks about,
and I was happy but wondered why
he looked sad. Inside, at home,
he cut my sandwich diagonally

instead of the right way, but it tasted better.
And I climbed into his lap to eat, to rest,
to touch the hands of a tool and die worker
embedded with slivers,

to trace the blue-veined swastika,
engraved by the fearful boys who didn't know German,
to find the lodged Korean shrapnel,
soon to be planted in American soil.

Now in my lap he asks me,
What will you remember when I'm gone?
And I reply, *The Father's Heart*
like the time you broke your leg.

Memory

Jenny Hanning

Once I saw a man stab another man. I watched one man put
a bread knife into the stomach of another man on a sidewalk
in Boston. I called 9-1-1 but could not name
the street. I was five steps from home, but didn't know my
address. I had to look for street signs. Everything took time.

The blondest of the three blond policemen was the first to
arrive. He was driving by in a quiet cruiser and pulled a U-
turn when he saw the blood running over the yellow curb.
Blood in the gutter—literally.

The others were less blond, later, older, and swung up
alongside us in a sucker-punch
of sound. The first officer picked up the knife and asked *Is
this the knife?* Blood was running down the blade. *Can you
describe the knife for me?* He was holding it away from his body.
He was an arm's reach away from me.

The stabbed man was twisting at our feet and the officer told
him *Settle down, sir.*

It was summer then, and then winter and I was summoned as
a witness, but I couldn't remember if there had been rain. I
didn't know what the men were fighting about, or if they had
been fighting at all.

The blondest policeman was there. He gave me a report to
read in the echoing hallway outside the courtroom. *Refresh
your memory* he said. While I tried to read he talked to me. He
told me about his daughter, Athena. *Named for the goddess of
mathematics,*
then paused and thought and added *War too. Everything you said*
he said *is right here.*
You just say it all again.

He told me how his wife dropped out of school when she got
pregnant and that he thought she should go back for her
degree, but she wanted to go to beauty school instead.
I said *Well everybody needs haircuts, right?* and I meant it kindly,
but the officer stopped talking with me then, and it was very
quiet.

The old window glass turned the falling snow the oddest
mossy green and it was so cold the marble benches became
patterned with layers of frost.

Finding

Jenny Hanning

I want it to be like the movies where we link hands and form
a net—
not for catching souls, but more like a giant moon bounce
made of fingers
and touching palms where the silhouettes of people gather
and
egg one another into the attempt of back-flips

When I was small—no—I'll be honest—I wasn't small at
all—
when I was a teenager I used to peel the loose bark off the
birches
and write myself desperate notes with the burned end of a
stick

I had these tiny china figurines
blue eyed spaniels and doll house maids with loose bending
joints—
pin-tiny holes strung through with hair thin wire
I wanted to bury them for someone else to find and did,
but after I'd done it I was terrified—
What if no one ever came digging?
So I unearthed them myself—

And later, dropped them at the rim of a shallow
duck pond in the public gardens
then drank coffee on a bench and watched
a pair of sisters point down into the water
then drop to their skun-over knees to fish them out—

And my boyfriends say it's mildly psychotic
to go around dropping things—
but there isn't any finding if there isn't any losing
and my ever favorite thing remains a brick
with the shape of running horse burned across it—

Besides, when the people renting the house up
on the hill packed up their hound-dogs and left
the double front doors were still
wide open and banging in the rain
and when I went up the hill to close them
I stepped through into the entryway instead
and saw the highest ceiling I'd even seen
and a cage full of canaries sitting on the floor
all their seed gone and their water cup empty

In the back garden it was like fairyland
with the moss eating out across the patio stones
and a lavender angora rabbit
stretched long and dying in its white iron hutch

Cutting the mats frees I sometimes
scissored accidental vs into
its soft and silver skin, but the rabbit never bled
and when I burned the last of the ticks out from
the insides of its ears the rabbit sighed
like a girl and rubbed its paws over its eyes
then nodded polite and aloof

So I named it Jack Speke for the explorer gentlemen
who might have said *I promise, Dick*, but lied, and later,
wedged a shotgun under his chin for the shame of it,
and then I let the rabbit loose to live

Notes

Laura Swindlehurst

In fifth grade your clarinet is stolen so you decide to pick up the saxophone. Your mother buys a Conn alto for $600 from an antique sale at a local mall. To you, the stars engraved on the horn look beautiful, but Mr. Jacob, the band director, will say you would've been better off renting a student instrument from Helmer's Music.

After feeling personally slighted by Mr. J., you protest vehemently that you will practice every day to compensate for the intonation problems he claims you and your inferior horn are causing his band. In spite of your efforts, he forbids you from playing a midrange D, a note which he says you are only allowed to finger until, finally, in eighth grade, you beg your mother and her new husband to shell out four grand for a beautiful new Yanigasawa alto saxophone. They will wrestle with you over it. It will take them five years to pay off. Swear up and down that you love band. Say you will definitely be playing through college, so it's a worthy investment.

Mr. Jacob dogs you until you become a rather fine musician.

Sit up straight.
Breathe from your diaphragm.
Don't pound on the reed with a fat tongue.
Keep your jaw forward.

You eventually take over as the second chair of the ninth grade band even though you are still in eighth grade.

52

Mr. J. says if you want any chance of becoming first chair next year you'd better go get yourself some private lessons because Sean O'Malley, the greasy haired boy that sits next to you, practices every night.

At this point, music has entered into your life in other ways. You listen to the radio constantly, holed up in your room, dreaming about how creative and unique you truly are. Write some poems. Beg your mom to buy you new CDs. Learn the lyrics to every song on the rock station until you know them all by heart. And always be opinionated with regard to your musical palette.

You've got the credentials to back you up now, so change the way you dress. Lose the silly t-shirts and overalls you've been sporting since seventh grade. Grow out your fluffy bangs. By ninth grade not only are you the first chair but you've got an army camouflage shirt and torn up jeans that Mom helped you tear. You like to think of yourself as an overachiever with an edge.

Mom gets angry with you now because you never want to put a coat on and you're wearing too much makeup for your age.

Find an instructor who will give you music lessons on the cheap. He will boast that he was once part of the official Disneyland marching band, and says that you will never have good tone unless your parents pay to have your jaw broken and reset. He tells you that a good saxophonist should look like a bulldog, an idea to which you are opposed. Tell him you hate Disneyland. Go home and examine your jaw. Quit your lessons after the second session.

You will decide to go with Mr. Bergich, the same instructor that pock-faced Sean O'Malley sees. In spite of wearing a hearing aid, he's the official bandleader of the National Guard. You'll be encouraged to join the armed forces. He'll say that you're a good saxophonist technically, but your playing really has no heart or feeling. Disagree with him in your mind. Go home puzzled over how to feel more.

You are also too reserved and you need to learn how to play jazz music. You think you hate jazz but agree to let Mr. Bergich teach you to play anyway.

High school arrives. Your best friend from ninth grade isn't your best friend anymore. The rocker clique at school will inform you that the music you listen to is pedestrian and rather lame. They say that punk rock is what's cool at Lincoln High, so you quickly forsake your old music collection and all the useless trivia you learned about music that nobody else seems to like.

Mr. Meyers will let you into his top concert band and ask you to do the jazz ensemble as well. You say no to the jazz band and then sit silently while your private instructor throws a fit and threatens to quit you. In the mean time you've become a punk rock elitist. Tell everyone the music they like sucks. Listen to all the bands your friends like and tell everyone how much you like them too, how much it speaks to you personally. At fifteen you may feel the need to fight the system although you're not entirely sure what that entails.

Join your friends' punk rock band Slaughter Regime as the saxophonist. Boys from other high schools will come and cheer you on. You aren't very good at making your own music because you don't know anything about improvising or chord progressions (because you didn't take jazz band), but no one seems to care so neither do you.

Cut your hair really short and spike it up. Start wearing all black every day. Apply purple eyeliner with a heavy hand before leaving for school. You join the jazz band even though you have to start school at 6:30 every morning. You want to be a better musician in case Slaughter Regime really starts going places. By springtime your band mates all hate each other and the band slowly dissolves. No one wants to say your group is broken up, but by now you've become a pretty good jazz musician.

Jazz it up all through junior and senior year and stick with the black thing. Sit in your room and listen to Dexter Gordon's ballads. A private instructor named Steven Carraway will call after the last concert of your senior year of high school because he heard you playing "Harlem Nocturne." He offers to teach you for free until you leave for college. He thinks you have a lot of potential.

Right off the bat he tells you that technically you are very good but you don't put much emotion into your playing. He tells you to go home and listen to some of his favorite jazz musicians and then try to copy them. You thought you were already playing with a great deal of emotion. He hurts your feelings. It doesn't seem to help.

Spend all summer learning a Charlie Parker song called "Donna." Technically it's probably the most difficult song you've ever played. You learn to play it at almost half the tempo that Bird did and it sounds horrible. And boring. And it's still hard. This is your audition piece for the University of Washington jazz ensemble.

Summer passes and you make Steven cookies to thank him for investing his time in you. Let him know you'll call him after your audition. For the first time, you've also got a boyfriend and now at eighteen you're fairly sure that you're in love with each other. After a month, on the day of your audition for the jazz ensemble, he'll break up with you and say that he only told you he loved you because that's what he thought you wanted to hear. Go to your audition early and listen to the other students before you play. They sound a lot better than you do, and you walk out before your name is called. Stick your saxophone in the closet in your dorm room. Run your hands over the leather case when you feel lonely, but don't play anymore.

Listen to the saddest music you know. Your roommate will complain that she's afraid you're trying to drive her to suicide. Move around slowly with your songs, like honey dripping from a heavy spoon. Say you feel bad when others ask how you've been, but try to look on the bright side, in some circles being miserable makes you cooler.

Once you're off campus and working, decide to teach yourself the guitar so you can write your own sad songs. Drone on about your emotional state while alone in your bedroom. Play a song you wrote to your friend, she'll tell you its "okay but kind of depressing." Tell her you have other songs. Play them. She'll say that they all sound "kind of the same."

Meet people who share your common interests, like sitting around being sad, listening to sad music. Change your musical taste to what they listen to. Tell your ex-boyfriend that you think Iron Maiden sucks now.

Forsake every song you ever liked. Authoritatively inform your friends of your new philosophy on how a musician's artistic vision is more important than mere lyrics or musical virtuosity. Listen to weird instrumental music nobody else likes for awhile, then give that up too.

Become such a music snob that you don't listen to any music at all anymore and listen exclusively to liberal talk radio. Decide it wasn't music that you loved so much after all, but music lyrics, which have been the poetry of your youth so far. Become an avid reader of literary classics. Keep your radio tuned to NPR. Take a beginning creative writing class the last quarter of your senior year of college.

Your classmates will tell you that your first story, which is about a barista who you have a crush on, is contrived and gimmicky. Don't rewrite it, toss it aside. Write more stories that are more or less about you. Show them to your friends until they are sick of reading them. Go home one day and kick your current boyfriend out of your apartment. Tell him you're moving on. He'll be taken back by your directness. He'll say that you're a real bitch. Don't bother with slamming the door in his face. Lock it quietly behind him as he leaves.

The World According to
Discover Magazine

Joe Pitkin

Sometimes I get tired
reading how horribly we're all going to die:
socked in by global warming, for instance,
everybody in water up to our necks
eating our own scabs and 20 year-old cans
of peaches bobbing along in the surf.

But who can you believe?
Two months later the cover
hums about how great life will be soon,
when no one is foolish anymore:
everyone eating enough fresh fruit,
Chilean grapes borne to us
by hydrogen blimp, or shot
into our homes from space, dozens of satellites
beaming fresh fruit and hip, youth-oriented music
from their geosynchronous rookeries.

Eventually one tires just as much
of reading that—it's not hard to see
how *Discover* is owned by
the Disney corporation, what with all
the Tomorrowland reveries about nano robots
dispatched into our veins, scrubbing away

unhygienic residues, wheedling us
to live for centuries, in the same issue with
some animated moralizing about Africanized bees
and how recklessly we brought stinging doom upon
ourselves.

Finally I fling this month's issue
across the room like a pack of smokes.
Take a breath: chances are
some non-bee fate
will get me in the end. The house is quiet,
no discernible buzzing, and the world works
the way it always did, journalists' and my
ignorance of the workings notwithstanding:
either life as a battle royale for apparently scarce resources—
either
that, or abundance teases us just beyond our field of vision.

The *Discover* jury remains deadlocked on that crucial question,
though look around and the living room
with the window on the garden
seems not to be awaiting any verdict, or, perhaps,
assumes the verdict is known: the squawking,
pugnacious scrub jays out in the yard
scrapping over a castaway ice cream sandwich,
the cantaloupe seedlings, stubborn, insistent heliotropes,
bound in their tiny yogurt cups, pressing their single
true leaves against the windowpane
like kids smooshing their noses into little snouts against the
glass.

Night Geese

Joe Pitkin

They may remember more than you believe.
They overflew this river long before
A city crowded each bank. From the shore
Toward the condoed floodplain, they achieve
What overflight they can now, as they leave
This brink no longer no one's anymore:
The honks fall softly, easy to ignore
In all the mash of noise these streets conceive.
A creature seeking in the open air
Keeps wider eye than one that lives within
A room: a goose will see what is beneath
Your dignity to notice. What is there
That feeds them still? What have they seen again
this season between verges lined like teeth?

Did others know?

H. L. Hix

She sent him one baby picture, enclosed with
only the briefest note: *Her eyes speak of you.*
As she herself had never been able to.
He kept it those fifty years, he keeps it still,
in the family album — the note kept, too,
but hidden — deflecting others' inquiries.
Her eyes speak of you who must be otherwise
hidden, here in me, there *as* her, in plain view.

Taking Candi From Her Babies

Nicole Ausmus

Clackamas Community College
Student Writing Contest Winner

My mother lies in a bed just twenty feet from me,
breathing with difficulty. Her breath changes from
hyperventilation to a tempo so sluggish I can't reproduce it
myself. I count: one, two, three.....up to thirty-five seconds
between gasps for oxygen. It can't possibly be sustaining her.
I watch numbers on the monitor: 120 over 80, 95 over 40.
She looks to me for reassurance that she is safe. I am doing
my best to comfort her, but I am sure that she can see
through my attempts. This place is teeming with medical
personnel, but we've told them "comfort measures only."
There will be no climactic saving of her life by the young
doctor, even though she is only forty-eight years old. There
are no false pretenses; we are waiting for her death. She and
us. Mother and children. One and three.

I don't have any idea what is waiting for her at death.
We know it is coming. She knows too, even though she can't
communicate that. She has known it for a while now, even
before she could bring herself to say the words. It is the one
thing that she can't forget or avoid.

My emotions hold me hostage, but I can only
recognize a few of them by name. Sadness, despair, anger,
exhaustion. Mostly I drift in an unfamiliar sensation, a feeling
foreign to me. I am grateful for this time, I tell myself. And I

62

really try to be. I am able to tell her that I love and cherish her, even though she can't reciprocate. I can put her hand to my face. There was a time when this hand was warm and soft, brushing stray hairs from my eyes or moving emphatically during the telling of a story.

I can't leave Hopewell House, the hospice facility. I have moved into her small room that faces a group of ancient rhododendrons, heavy with blossoms ready to expand. Some are red, some dark pink. I wonder if she will see them in full bloom, if she has that much time. I have clothes for a week, a toothbrush, and a small, framed picture of my husband and daughter. I miss them. But I can't leave. I have to be here every moment, due to my own anxiety and purpose. I need to be here to talk for her. And to her. Also because I am her medical liaison, but mostly for the guilt I feel over Grandpa. I promised him I would stay with him.

*

I had been caring for Grandpa every day for over four months, and I was feeling drained. With very few family members still living and capable, and my mother terminally ill, there was only me. A few paid hospice nurses, and me. I needed a break from the pain and meds and fear and impending death. My family wanted to go away to do something fun, to try and feel like normal people again. We decided to take a short trip to Seattle to visit some friends. I felt it risky to leave Grandpa, but his nurses assured me that he was doing okay and that we would be safe to leave for a couple of days. "Besides, if he starts to go downhill, we will call you, and you are only a couple of hours away," the nurse encourages. "You'll have time to get back to be with him if things take a turn."

But we didn't have time. We left late on a Friday, and Saturday was spent working out medication changes and

63

filling in the gaps of home hospice care schedules while my husband and daughter played video games. Every time the phone rang, I panicked. I'm on edge. I shouldn't have gone.

Late Saturday night, as I was getting ready for bed, I felt a sudden urge to call Grandpa's to check in. I'd been on the phone with his nurse just two hours earlier, but I felt an urgency to call that wasn't there before. The sound of her voice instantly tells me that things are not well. "Oh Nicole," she says desolately, "Your Grandpa just passed away, not even five minutes ago. He's gone." I should have been there.

I had been on autopilot for so long that I hadn't grasped that he was really going to die. I hadn't had any time to shed tears. But as soon as she said the words, I looked around my friend's guest room, and knew that this was not where I was supposed to be. I had promised I would be there. He was with a stranger when he took his final breath. My emotions spilled over.

We leave immediately, even though the nurse insists I should get some rest. She promises nothing will happen before I get there in the morning. I know I won't sleep.

The cremation arrangements need to be made right away. My mom has scheduled a meeting time with the company that my Grandpa had chosen. We are the only car in the parking lot. It is very early Sunday morning.

"Just have me cremated and throw my ashes in the garbage. I don't want a fuss," he had said a few weeks before. My mom and I had protested loudly, exactly the reaction he had been looking for.

We walk through the door, and the bells on the knob ring softly. It is my first time going through this process, at least from this perspective. The room is cramped and stagnant, the air doesn't move. I look in a glass display case as we wait. My heart breaks at the sight of tiny urns adorned with baby blocks and rattles. I am suddenly very aware that this is a business attempting to turn a profit. I feel a flare of anger towards this company for selling these items. How could they give a sales pitch at such a time? I would never be able to do that job, I think.

Even though I am weary and my brain is moving slowly, I am able to give the funeral home clerk the information she needs for Grandpa's death certificate, his social security number, his address, numbers that I know by heart. After this meeting, I will only need to recite them a few more times. The official causes of death are Lymphoma and complications due to Chronic Obstructive Pulmonary Disease, COPD. It seems too brief a summary after the intense pain and suffering that he went through.

My mother's hands tremble as she signs the order, and it does not go unnoticed. The clerk pats her hand and offers a sympathetic look, a look that I have come to know very well.

As we leave the building, I try to be strong. Mom is already so stressed. She's been battling nausea for months now, a byproduct of chemotherapy and an intestinal blockage. The last thing I want her to feel is that she needs to comfort me. After all, it is her father who's died.

A little less than two months later, it is Mom in the same position, looking death in the face. I don't know how to feel or the right way to grieve. I can't get a grip on a particular emotion. I don't even know who I am. I am this person, floating around the halls at the hospice center, making decisions for the woman who had always made the decisions for me. I am the too-thin woman, surviving on day-old pastries donated by a local Starbucks and three Venti lattes a day. I am twenty-six years old. I don't have a point of reference for any of this. I am not sure that anything I am doing is right.

I try to talk to Mom, because she's always had the answers, but she is gone for all intents and purposes. Morphine flows easily into her veins through an IV, at doses so high that her awareness has departed. A nurse tells me Mom can still hear me, that I should keep talking, but I don't see any indications of what made her my mom anymore. She is barely a sliver of a woman in this bed, skin yellowed and leather-like, stretched tight over bones, eyes milky and hollow, with scarce tufts of auburn hair.

God, please let this end. Let her stop suffering, I cry at night, in a cot beside her bed, the covers pulled over my head. *But please don't let her die. I can't be without my mom. My daughters need their Grandma.* My prayers are impossible to answer. I can't have it both ways.

The door opens every few hours, so the nurses can check her medication pump and catheter. "That colon cancer...an awful thing," the attending nurse mumbles. She has seen it before, but it is new to me. My skin is covered in hives. "A by-product of stress," the nurse comments. A sympathetic orderly gives me a Benedryl out of her purse, and I achieve three hours of tortured sleep.

I wake to her screams, urgent and devastating, screams that the doctor can't figure a reason for. The monitor next to her bed shrieks in warning. A drip of Valium quiets the room once more, except for the audible sound of my racing heart. *God, please let her go.*

Then, suddenly, at 11:41 p.m. on a Thursday night, He does.

*

Two months after her death, I realize that my memories of her face are fading. My grief flares, as intense and bright as ever. The pictures on the wall look back at me like someone I once knew, rather than the woman closest to me. I never thought that I would see a day when I would start to forget my mother. When someone isn't physically there everyday, details blur in a mechanism of emotional self-defense.

I can't even begin to describe the hole in my heart. I have no idea what to do to fill it.

A few weeks ago we went to Roaring River campground, nestled near the base of Mt. Hood, a place our family calls "The Spot." It's where my mom wanted her ashes scattered, there with my dad, and three of the dogs we'd owned over a lifetime.

My husband, daughter, and I met my brother and his girlfriend, and my sister and brother-in-law late in the afternoon. We planned to camp out for a night, to enjoy each other and the forest, but the trip was shrouded by the real purpose of the excursion. We were there to leave my mom's remains, which were wrapped in a paper bag in the car, a bag my husband had placed behind the driver's seat, a bag that I couldn't bring myself to look at. I know it is stamped with her name. Candace.

I drank a lot that night. I couldn't stand the feel of my own skin. Thank God my husband was there to keep things together because I was of no use. I don't know how much I drank. I laughed, cried, made jokes, and carried on until early in the morning. But the next day, I felt surprisingly well, and I was ready for the two and a half mile hike to "The Spot."

When we arrived, everyone was hot and sweaty. The temperature in the high 80's at least. My husband and brother-in-law decided to cool down in the river. Our energy is warm and positive. When I take a place on a large rock to start the impromptu ceremony, everyone falls silent.

I clear my throat and it hits me all at once. I have to stand there for a couple of minutes, waves of emotion pass through me. I am hoping that I can handle this last obligation.

I began to read "The River Doesn't Know We Call It River," or "No sabe el rio que se llama rio," a piece that I

67

found on Mom's laptop, labeled "Read This When You Scatter My Ashes." She'd had it all planned out. She wanted this piece to be read, so I would read it. The rushing sounds of the river were a fitting backdrop to the words of Benjamin Alire Sáenz:

> We divide time into years. We divide years into seasons. We have different names for every river, a different name for every ocean of the Earth. The river doesn't know we have named it "river," it does not know that it is separate from the waters that call "Come." River, I have been gone a long time. I am returning to your waters. River, I've come back. River, I am afraid. Carry me like water.

When I finish reading, I clutch the bag close to my heart for a few moments, and begin to release what was left of my mom's physical body into the river. After, I lift her towards the rushing waters, and watch as the gray powder hits, swirling and rushing between rocks. My breath caught in my mouth, I couldn't speak. All I can do is pass Mom to my sister, the middle child, next in line.

My sister throws the ashes in one fluid motion, sending her portion of Mom abruptly into the river. She extends her arm out to reach my brother, who is standing on another rock close to the middle of the river. He had been standing on this rock with a distant look on his face, no tears, no smiles. He takes Mom out of my sister's hands, and slowly, carefully, lets Mom slip into the water. He's saved just a bit at the bottom of the plastic bag for my daughter.

She wasn't expecting this honor. She was busy throwing little rocks into the water, only marginally paying attention to the rest of us. Her eyes widened as I approached, and let the little collection of pebbles in her hands fall to the ground. She chose a spot close to the bank of the river, and let the remaining ashes gather on top of a flat rock. She swirls her finger through them, interested.

"It's my special rock for Grandma," she says, looking up at me.

"That's right," I say, my eyes wet. "Now, when you come back, you always have a special place to talk to Grandma. She will always be here."

"But how come I can't see her, or hear her?"

"You can!" I say brightly to my daughter. "Listen to the water. Isn't it loud? Grandma's voice isn't quite as loud as the water, so you really have to listen hard to hear her."

We sit there together, her small hand folded in mine, listening to the water.

"I hear her!" She exclaims after a few moments. "But I can't tell what she's saying."

"It sounds like 'I love you so much,'" I say. "And I know she's talking to you. She's loved you since the moment she saw you born into the world."

Enough explanation for her, she smiles luminously and carefully places pebbles around the ashes. My daughter is beautiful and trusting. I wish there were an answer that simple for me.

When we return to the camp, I want to leave immediately. The feeling is so intense, I long for my home and familiar bed. I hastily pack our supplies, loading the car carelessly.

After a quick goodbye, we begin the journey home. As soon as we turn onto the highway, I am flooded with both relief and regret. I'd left my mother, now swirling in the cold river, bound for the waters of the sea. The sun is high in the sky, the trees green and tall, and the river fast and glimmering. My daughter talks a blue streak in the backseat, my husband fiddles with the radio, and I choke back tears as we leave my heart behind.

Sáenz, Benjamin Alire. "No Sabe el rio que se llama rio."
    Dark and Perfect Angels. El Paso: Cinco Puntos, 1995.
    Print.

Civil Works
Dave Seter

Just out of college I learned to work,
to turn textbook theory into practice.
Blueprint, spreadsheet, jackhammer,
the gas company taught me a thing or two.
New engineers joined the work crews
of unionized men who tore up the streets
listening for hissing gas. Equations
taught me how much force concrete could take,
but up close it's dirty work, opening the street.
New Jersey's covered ten inches deep
in Depression era concrete, tough
make-work stuff. My boss of the spreadsheet
never drove out to join us, never knew
how the work day happened, or started.
Every morning the crew assembled a cooler
full of bottled beer to haul rattling along
and drink when the job was done.
It's no joke—experienced laborers really
use their beer guts—to balance the weight
of pavement breakers, forty pounds each
and bucking with compressed air. With each
clatter and kick of the jackhammer's blade,
I realized why workmen curse. Civil works
are more than just blueprints—but also
wordless gestures—even uncivil words.

An Unexpected Succession
of Light

Patrick Carrington

I

As a boy I watch men sweat and harvest,
their skin like lanterns in the sun—

my eyes love the sting of silver on the silos
where they store beans
until they get their price, the sly wink

from the hinges of the barn
where the dirty girls
of town will come to drop their pants

at night. Everything
in me wants to know what sparkles.

II

Loneliness loved long enough becomes a lamp.

I can see the day breathe deep to sing
and forget the words,

watch a wind in late afternoon
whistle its dirge and dance
the funeral stomp.

III

As clouds gather and night creeps in
with its black cape, I eye
the sky and leave
my testament under hell's starless roof—
When I am discovered by a child
or whore or farmer planting,
waste no fanfare on me,

save your sweat for the corn.
Toss me in a fruit cart,

over a saddle. Fertilize the field
with me if times are hard.

Wash my smell from your hands.

Three Pigs

Rodney Gomez

The wolf plies the first pig with a fat cauldron of mud
but the pig doesn't bite, never having known pleasure,
and the nearby spit is too much like the prod he felt
in childhood, when he and a hundred other hooves
were so compressed they had to breathe in unison.

The second pig is almost convinced by the wolf's ode
to Darwin, and wonders how bad it could possibly be
to find a home in the stomach of a carnivore,
and don't millions do it every day? Then he recalls
how hard it is to read Spencer in an acid bath.

The third pig takes his skin off and lays it in the yard—
shield and holster and blue fabric—then renounces
his code, since he sees in the wolf's eyes an angle
of himself in a lawless life. Naked, he opens
the window: if not to die, then at least to make love.

The Wheeled Woman

Meagan Cass

Come spring this dead end strip of concrete in the middle of Central Park will crowd with men and women roller dancing, their skin shining, their moves fluid and mirthful. A DJ will play hip hop and disco, and there will be hot dog vendors and pretzel vendors, the smells of sweat and salt. Teenage boys in baggy pants will wind through strands of cones and grind on benches, their trucks flashing in the afternoon sun, and older men will court tottering new girls in flimsy Reidels, coaxing them into the fray as they blush and giggle. Ice cream cones will melt and spill on our surface.

But today, in the cold December quiet, there is just a middle aged couple in quads and matching leather jackets and me, circling them in smooth crossovers, stalking. I watch their bodies knot and unknot in the fading light. The woman regards me warily as I circle, as if fearing I might steal her man, hook him with the rail of my arm and skate him away to devour the warm bread of his heart.

"How you doing?" I say brightly, smiling as I pass them, cutting so close to their boring waltz that I can smell her perfume and his cologne.

Yet there is no joy, really, in this kind of play, and I leave the strip, knife my way through the winter trees toward Fifth Avenue, joining the rhythmic, purposeful rush downtown, toward the night clubs. Tonight I will pound the tequila shots they give me for free because I am on skates, then stand at the bar with my hip cocked and let men and women whip me around, let them pull me close then twist me away, threatening to send me hurtling into the smoky darkness. The risk will almost make me happy. My hands will stay cool in their sweaty hands. My body will be dry and hard as they turn messy and wet and pliant. Every night it is this way.

Once, I lived in a blue house with good wooden floors, tucked into the mountains of Binghamton, in upstate New York. I lived with a man, a husband, who loved me. I had thick, soft thighs and soft heavy arms then, and I moved slowly in pilly sweaters and flat soled boots in winter, in billowy peasant skirts and floral hippy shirts in spring. He taught high school earth science, and Saturday mornings we would go hiking through the hills at dawn, collecting rocks and fossils, him retelling the story of how our mountains were once covered with ocean, our world once immersed, home to sea creatures.

"Imagine we are under water," he would say, sweeping his arm across the hills and valleys and the hard red brick of Binghamton's small downtown.

Saturday nights I would ball up on the couch with a novel, still for hours while he graded papers or practiced his clarinet. He had played as a boy and didn't want to lose his talent. These nights, I loved when the temperature dropped below zero, and the sky bellowed wind and snow, and I could hear the persistent rows of his music—he preferred Mozart—neatly parceling out our time. When he was through we would make love, looking at each other, and the house would seem to fit us perfectly then.

Children liked me, during these years. I taught first grade, and at recess they would come to me, hoisting themselves onto my knees, the girls gushing their crushes and tiffs, the boys sputtering how they'd been bullied. I loved their easy, trusting affection. My own mother had been a mean, beautiful woman, a singer in a rock band who had married my father young, gave up music and, in her words, got all "Jesusy" like him. Then when I was twelve she picked up music again, left my father and I with her new band to go travel the world. Left forever. I grew up with my father's stern warnings: if I wasn't careful I would grow up selfish and harsh like her. He threw out all her things and moved us to a rotting house on the edge of the city, where he ate lots of fried food and died of a heart attack when I was eighteen. As an adult, I liked the idea of myself as firm and hospitable, more solid than either of them, a structure of a woman that would hold, nurturing.

We were discussing the prospect of our own children, the husband and I, the night before the skates appeared. "You're so good with them," he was saying.

It was a Saturday, early August, the trees in the hills heavy and tired looking with abundance. We had just come home from a hike and he was pacing excitedly, the way he always did when he came in from the outdoors.

I sat at the kitchen table watching his big hands move through the air. It was a conversation we had been having for a year. I told him I had never been mothered myself, as he well knew. I might not know how to do it. I might be bad at it. I didn't think I wanted to.

"You're so grounded," he said, sitting and putting a thick arm around me, rising back up. "You'd be fantastic," he said. "Please," he said.

I thought about how shaky he'd been when we'd met, at a night pottery class in the city. He had been a new teacher, twenty-two, gaunt and lonely and addicted to energy pills, his hands stuttering over the damp clay. My casseroles and biscuits and our long walks through the hills had steadied him. Now here he was, his face still flushed with exercise, standing in front of me on two strong legs, asking.

I told him that *yes* this was something we could do.

In the morning I found them in my closet, buried beneath my loafers like some bold new kind of house pests, their long, smooth tongues lapping up at me, the rusted metal of the wheel bearings winking in the dark. I picked them up, tugged their hot pink laces, ran my fingers over the dark, red leather, spun the translucent wheels with my palm. They made a dull, whirring sound, like the insides of conch shells.

At first I didn't recognize them as my own.

"What the heck?" I said to my husband, holding them up. I never cursed back then.

"Let me see them," he said. I let them fall from my hands onto the bed.

He laughed. "So all we need are some bell bottoms and Diana Ross. Try them on."

I played with the stiff tongues. I shoved my feet in. My toes cramped. The leather jabbed at my ankles. I sucked in my breath, took one, two thrusts forward, banging my knee on the bed but loving the airy gush the wheels made on the wood floor.

"Bravo!" he shouted.

I smiled, did a clumsy bow. This really was a great new game.

I lurched toward the door, barreled into the hall, where I lost my balance and slammed into the map of Binghamton we'd had framed. It fell and the glass broke over the floor.

My husband was there instantly, his arms around me. "You okay? Alright? Sweetheart?"

I looked down at the skates, two rounded nubs beneath my pants, the pink front breaks like clown noses. It was then that I noticed the tiny scuff mark on the right skate, from the one time I'd worn them at twelve. I remembered a certain Saturday afternoon at the Binghamton Rock and Skate, my hands hitting the waxed floors, the dizzy, Kylie Minogue humiliation of it. *Come on baby, do the locomotion.* My mother had brought me three months before she would leave forever, a last ditch effort to bond with this meek, quiet daughter who spent all weekend tunneled in Victorian coming of age novels. Skating was a thing my mother had loved as a girl. This would be fun!

Leaning on my husband, I made it back to the bed and shucked the skates off, threw them back into the dark of the closet. The stupid things. I did not care to remember that time, the way my mother had tried to guide me before I fell, her long red finger nails digging into my arm, saying, "Bend your knees, what are you a mannequin?" How I had then escaped to the Rock and Skate snack bar for french fries and a coke. I did not care to remember the silence of our car ride home, the silence that would follow her leaving, the cottony silence of abandonment that filled my father's house, muffling all of our small joys.

Outside the morning sky was a robin's egg blue, the hills a lush patchwork of green. I cleaned up the glass, spooned tuna fish salad on brown bread for our lunches. When a piece of glass I'd missed cut into the tough skin of my heel, I winced, but did not cry out.

And for weeks I forgot about them, the skates, though everything I did felt vaguely off-kilter. I went to school and gave my classroom a thorough cleaning, dusted all the glass apple paperweights that had accumulated on my desk. At home I paged through the phonebooks thinking of baby names, my vision blurring in the lines of small print. In the evenings I could not stop eating: packaged snack cakes, frozen pizzas, whole loaves of bread spread thick with butter.

"Are you already, or is there a marathon coming up?" my husband asked me, brushing crumbs from my nightgown in bed.

"It's too early to tell," I snapped, some new, dull anger rising in my voice. I was already two weeks late, had noticed a new tenderness around my nipples, but I thought I might keep this a secret awhile. I wasn't ready to say the word "pregnant" out loud. I thought of my mother, in her leather pants and cowboy boots, getting pregnant with me. I wondered, had it been this way for her?

The first day of school the children repeated my name at all once, calling me back to my life, my routine. At recess they were already upon me, encircling me with their bony arms, whispering secrets into my ears with their milky breath. My skin felt hot, their fingers like tiny match sticks.

Hiking that Saturday, I tired quickly, my body slow and heavy. The cut from the glass would not heal, and remained a steady, even pain. While I sat on a rock, my husband collected sprigs of honey suckle and stuck them in my hair and said, "You look like the goddess of spring," and I laughed though what I really wanted was for him to shut up and lead us home.

That night, lying awake next to him, the cool night air blooming out our windows, I slipped out of bed. I threw on shorts and a t-shirt. What I wanted was to slink out of my body, to feel the fresh wind of that motion for just a minute. I opened the closet door. They looked startled and feral in the dark, the red leather striped with moon light. I put them on, sucked in my breath and thrust forward. Thrust and glide and I was in the hall. Then I was doing an awkward kind of cabaret down the stairs. Then I was out the door and on the street, the hills engulfing me in a calm, velvety dark. I carved slow switchbacks down the long hill of our street, almost screaming with the rushes of speed, the night air washing over me, the chunky pavement vibrating through my bones.

My thighs ached, then burned. I picked my way across the Susquehanna Bridge into the small, rusted downtown, tripping over potholes, the pavement pressing red stars into my elbows and hands. My feet started to hurt but I didn't want to go home yet, knew, by some instinct, that I would not be able to sleep. On Main Street I hunkered past the crush of beefy sorority boys and sleek sorority girls in heels, feeling like a girl King Kong hulking her way through the delicate world of men. I stumbled over discarded pizza crusts and beer cans. I knocked into one of the girls and fell onto my knees and she brushed gravel from her tiny dress and said, "Fucking watch it, bitch." The lights of the cop cars parked outside the bars cut into my eyes. My feet were on fire.

Fearing I might come apart right there on the street, I hauled myself home. I took the skates off on the stoop, ran a bath filled with mineral salts and soaked my sore feet until they cooled. I put the skates away again and slid into bed beside him. When he blinked awake, looking vaguely annoyed, I told him I had just been on a night walk. He went back to sleep. He was a nervous man, a worrier, and this night I didn't feel like explaining myself. I turned and turned in bed. So I had two secrets now, from the man I loved. I decided, pulling him into me, that I was done skating.

Yet slowly they seduced me. While he made love to me my bare feet tingled, wanting the hard brace of the leather. The bed was hot and claustrophobic, my body heavy and spreading in it. The skates seemed to beckon. The next night I went further and stayed out later, made it all the way to the Rock and Skate at the Northern edge of the city. The giant dome of it glowed luridly in the night, though the parking lot was empty. It was almost exactly as I remembered it—the smell of stale popcorn, the purple rink surface lit with neon fluorescent lights, a huge disco ball

81

hanging from the ceiling, on the far walls a mural of a cartoon boy and a girl skating, their cartoon eyes wide with joy. Except that there was a only this woman in here, in leather pants and a red corset and a long braid of grey hair, doing small turns in the middle, humming to herself, something, I thought, by Patsy Cline. And it was freezing in here.

"Hello?" I shouted.

The woman abruptly stopped turning. Her eyes were bright green chips in her pale face. "Who's there and what do you want?" she said, and in three quick glides she was at the rink door, looking me up and down.

"Just browsing," I said. I laughed at myself.

"No one comes just to browse, doll face," she said and cackled.

She wore silver lipstick and silver eye shadow, and her breath smelled of cigarette smoke. She looked to be about fifty, the age my mother would be.

"Come here," she said, gesturing with her hand.

I wanted to leave; I did not like how she looked at me, like she knew me. But my skates seemed to move beneath me as if by their own volition, like dogs waiting to be let out. I gave her my hand.

And then she was moving me in fast circles around the rink, twisting me into full and half turns, telling me to bend my knees, to arch my back. She let go my hands and looped around me, brushing me with her sharp, angular shoulders, nearly knocking me over. The lights of the rink seemed to get brighter and hotter and I could feel that cut on my heel pulsing but I kept going, until I was sweaty and out of breath. I took off my pilly sweater. I jammed my hair into a bun. I mirrored her graceful arms, her hard, steady thrusts, the way she jutted her chin out like a hunter. Round and round I went, this woman beside me, neither of us speaking. I was thinking of my mother, what she would make of this scene, her matronly, married daughter sweating it out at the

Rock and Skate. She would probably be pleased. She would shake her head, the woman I used to know, and say, "That a girl." The thought bothered me. I didn't want to do anything in my adult life that would please her. If she had appeared just then and smiled at me, still young, the woman who had torn away from my life, I would have elbowed her in the stomach.

"Come back soon," the woman said when I was so tired I could barely stand.

"We'll see," I said.

At home I found him on the couch waiting. I stood before him, my head bent, drenched in sweat, my muscles quivering with exhaustion.

"You smell like god damn smoke," he said. I shuddered. He hadn't gotten this angry with me since the faculty party back in June, when I had stayed out late and brought a group of the younger teachers over to drink beer and play truth or dare. He did not like it when I drank, said it made me a more aggressive person, took me out of myself.

"You should be more careful now, shouldn't you?" he said meaningfully.

"I don't know," I said, though I was almost a month late now.

"How can you not know?"

"I mean, I'm not yet," I said. "I'm sorry," I said. "I'll stop," I said, hearing the weak tin of resolve in my voice. Drug addicts, I figured, must speak this way.

"Okay," he said, crumpling back down on the couch. "Okay." And when he made love to me that night, his hands held firm on my hips, pressing me into the bed, and when it was over he lay on top of me for awhile, the solid, warm girth of him shifting now and then until I pushed him off.

***

83

And I could not stop. During the days there was an odd numbness in my feet like the beginnings of frostbite. I floated in front of my students, going through the lessons I'd given the last five years by rote. Their names would not stick to my mind, and each morning I made up name tags with a red sharpie. They stared at me suspiciously as I affixed them to their sweaters, as if they were prison tags, their desks small cells.

At recess, when they came to me, I pulled them off, pinching at the soft skin of their bellies and saying, "I am not your mother." In this way they learned to fear me.

I began to stay out later and later, through the flushed ripening of October and into November's uneven bursts of cold. My thighs hardened. My legs became stippled with small scars. Soon I could glide steadily, could get up some speed. I would slink inside as the sky was turning from black to indigo, shower, rub tiger balm on my feet to soothe the burning, then slide into bed, whispering that I'd been walking, walking, in the cold night.

"My sweet girl," he would say, rolling over, thinking, I guess, that maybe I was pregnant, that this was just a crazy thing a pregnant lady might do, like eating dirt.

I thought in winter the cold would sooth my desire but it only intensified it. I skated the scabby, uneven paths flanking the river, braved the thin shoulder of Vestal Parkway to the smooth parking lots of the new chain stores across from the University, loving the harsh cold of the air.

"You're looking gorgeous, sweet pea," the woman in the rink said, her green eyes flashing, her silver star earrings shaking as she did quarter turns so precise they were like things that could cut you. "You better be careful here. You might never want to leave. That's how I got here," she said.

And sometimes, on the long skate home, I would catch sight of myself in the darkened storefront windows of the shops downtown and see a rangy looking girl and think of

84

my mother the month before she left, how she had stopped eating anything but anchovies and olives, how my father and I would find empty bottles of whiskey out on the lawn, how there had been the same deep, purple shadows around her eyes.

"You smell like sheep and rotting onions," one of my first graders said to me the day before and it was true. I had stopped showering, skating a kind of molting.

But I had spent too much of my life listening to warnings. I was enjoying living a life as two separate women: the house woman, flat footed, making meals and loving a man, and the night woman in tank tops and v-necks that cut deep into my chest, which I bought at a store called Forever 21 that had pulsing club music and lots of younger girls in it. I replaced my translucent wheels with a pair of sleek black Cobras. At the rink, with the strange, witching woman, I would think of my mother on stage. The year before she left us she played lead in a band called Kitten Whip, and once she'd snuck me into one of her shows without telling my father. She had stood in the lights sweating and leaning into her guitar. She snarled at the audience. Her anger shook me, a more vivid, artful version of the anger that raged at my father and his prudishness back at the house. At home she had yelled. At the concert, her voice was a smashed beer bottle shot through with light. I was terrified and overcome with love for her.

Spring broke hard on my husband and me. Melting ice pulled blocks of concrete loose and spilled them across my path. Ice storms turned the mountain roads slick as eels. Coming home from the rink one night I broke an arm, and all of the students signed my cast, one by one, carefully, as if, at any moment I might go wild and bite them.

At home we fucked in the kitchen, me bent over the counter, his hands trying to still my moving hips, me turning and kissing him all teeth, trying to draw blood from those red lips. He would want to pour thick, mud over me, I knew by the way his hands sculpted, held, pressed. He was mountains, and long winters, and thick forests, and heavy, damp snow. I was oil slicks and car horns and the casual raucous of streets in New York, a city my mother said she had played gigs at once, a city I had never been to but, already, felt drawn to. He held and I bit, he clenched and I shifted. And through the rainy, muddy, maw of the season this was the dance we danced, the dance of two geographies each trying to overtake the other.

When he played his clarinet in the evenings I told him to can it, I could barely hear myself think. The ashy taste of cruelty filled my mouth, and I learned to love the pain of the boots, felt like I deserved it.

He stopped asking about the baby.

I stopped changing my clothes, settling into a tight t-shirt and a pair of jeans cut at the ankles to accommodate the skates. The t-shirt grew wet, then dry, then wet with my sweat, the fabric fading and turning thin. The bottoms of the jeans frayed and dragged luxuriantly across the floors of our house. My hair shone with grease and my nails grew long and yellow and curled, making it hard to hold a pencil at school, to wrap my arms around him without breaking the skin.

It was increasingly painful to take the skates off every night, and to walk in the world on foot, short and slow and grounded. My ankles craved inward. My legs turned weak. My feet were small, bleached fists in my shoes. The children moved so quickly, in packs. I feared they would seize me with their small hands, smelling my hatred and fear of them like dogs. My husband seemed to grow larger and taller, his arms and legs like tree trunks. He forced me on long, Saturday hikes, saying, "You skate so much, you should be in shape for this."

I began to leave the skates on all day, first only at work, and then at home too. At work, the children and the other teachers found this charming.

"Wooee," the children shouted when I glided into their classroom.

But they quickly turned wary.

Blisters rose and popped on my heels, and at the seam between skate and calf. Our house became one of squalor, caked with mud and water he tracked in with his boots, and gravel come loose from my wheels. He took long hikes every day now, without me, or shut himself in the music room, which was to be the nursery.

And I spent less and less time inside. In the house, in my skates, I tended to break things: glasses, mugs, picture frames. I kicked over his potted plants, and the dry, parched soil spilled over the floor. I ruined a vase we had made in that pottery class we met in.

In the house we moved defensively around each other, our shoulders hunched, each unsure how to judge the distances between the other. I began sleeping on the couch—he didn't want me in bed with those machines, he said—then not sleeping at all, spending the long, curve of the night at the rink. My skating became faster, harder, harsher. Outside I felt better, the cold wind clawing my bare arms and neck, the mass I felt in the womb loosening, my feet twisting and throbbing. Some nights I skated so long, my stomach hollowed with hunger, I feared I might immolate, become movement itself, a glint of a girl on the edges of people's memories.

Then, one morning in April, I woke in the morning and skated outside under a hard, gray sky and my feet no longer hurt. I was light. The thing inside me was gone. I skated into town and home again, the wind blowing my hair back behind me. I took a shower and felt the hot water on the leather, sentient.

It was a Saturday. He was playing his clarinet, scales, over and over again, the notes like bars on a window. "If you can't stay still," he shouted from behind the closed door, "why don't you get the hell out?"

I did. I coursed through my city with a new impatience, past the abandoned storefronts and factories of downtown, past the decrepit colonials from the city's industrial heyday, through every single potholed street, the sky growing dark and the air cooling, an icy rain beginning. I found the rink dark, the doors locked, which did not surprise me. There was no more work to be done there. What I wanted, alone and newly strange and unnerved in the cold dark, was to undo it. The change was a curse I had cultivated. This body could not be my own. I raced home, faster than I should have in that weather, the city a crumbling, burnt out car of a place, the trees clattering with wind, the hills rocking around me.

At the house all of the lights were on. Towers of his books were piled on all the tables, and in the brightness I could see the cobwebs in the corners, the plant soil still on the floor, bits of food on the rug. I realized we had been living like animals. The good wooden floors were covered with long, black streaks from my wheels, like the letters of a language neither of us could decipher. "I'm leaving," he said.

I skated up to him, towering over him in his t-shirt and jeans, hating how powerful I felt above him. I bent to tried and kiss him but he bristled.

"Help me take them off," I said.

"Why?" he said.

"They won't stop," I said. "I want to stop," I heard myself say.

He knelt beside me, unsmiling, his hands steady. I lifted my right foot onto his thick thigh and he worked to untie the first skate. When he pulled at the laces I winced, started sweating. Our lamps flickered—we had stopped

88

changing the bulbs weeks ago. He pulled back the tongue of the boot, hard. I clenched my fists. He said, "Don't move."

I said, "Be gentle."

He said, "I'm trying."

I said, "Go slow."

He said, "What the hell do you think I'm doing?"

But it was no use. I jerked forward, said, "Get the fuck hell off." I scratched at those soft hands, the hands of the man I had loved, with my nails, wanting to get at the smooth, red skin of his arms, to get at his bones.

For a moment I pulled at the trucks myself, pretending to try to unlock the secret but knowing, the knowledge like the pit of some new fruit lodged in my chest, that I did not want to find it.

He stood up and looked at me, his face so far away, so old, so tired and I could tell that he knew, too.

Outside, the rain grew louder. We each looked at our feet, mine rolling back and forth, his bare and planted on our dirty floor. We looked up at each other. What can you say, in love, when one person has become another creature?

I burst from the box of the house into the damp, icy night. From our hill I could see the blurry lights of downtown, could hear the calm, steady roar of Highway Eighty-One veining south to the Thru-way, to the Taconic's deadly curves. I was exhausted but I kept going, pushing, thrusting out of the rain. People honked and shook their heads inside their cars but I was undaunted. The miles of darkness flew, the mountains dark things behind me until morning came and I was in Central Park, in the middle of the lima bean loop. A group of bikers in blue spandex raced past me soundlessly, surrounding me like a school of tropical fish.

I stood there for a moment, lungs heaving, the sky a blood red warning sky. I thought of the place I had left. I wondered how and in what ways I would miss him. Then I realized I was starving and it was bitter cold and there were so many streets here and I pushed, forward, again, towards where the people were.

Driving Drunk, and a
Dozen White Crosses

Lisa Fay Coutley

from her purse to her palm. She revs her cemetery
      toward a gauzy daymoon, curves our Buick

the hipbend home. Mouthfuls of ditch flowers
      purple and passing, cottonwoods spilling

that moon's confetti, the coal in Mother's eyes
      whitening. This is the fire I warm my hands by.

Clear the deadwood, and you'll see, nothing but a girl
      with a mouth dry of music. Let's pretend

this is thirst, when a girl might stagger three, maybe four
      days before paving her own mirage: a single drop

of oil down a harp string. Rain. Under this influence,
      it will take years to learn she's a room she drags

with her. Wall-to-wall nettles she's shaped into banjos,
      maracas, a flute. When it finally comes time to sit

to the river, she'll have to finger her throat, snap in halves
      all the notes that woman sung into her—

granite specks from hammer to chisel to headstone—
    until the horse in her heart stamps its hooves again.

Sweet Blood

Wendy Willis

for Ruby

Because you said desire
smells like corn
and lured the yearling shadows
close enough to nuzzle,
we called you deer whisperer.

Because you hiccupped as the incense ball
neared, we poured salt
in the furthest corner of the yard.

Because you called out
the hummingbird's secret,
we learned to split
the baby and glue splinters
back to bark. For those graces,
you'll pay in cinnamon and cabbages.

And though I don't remember whose arms
I abandoned as you mewled
at the old maid's wedding, it was not
a single-grained silence
shattered, but an invocation
of mermaids' hair and buck teeth.

Because I held you in my hand
like a watermelon seed, an amulet
against late summer's backward glances,
you could not be passed one apron
to the next. Your just-finished skin,

thin as grapeskin, draped your sweet
blood as your father and I faced
one another to begin our last mantra
and I cried your name in a gasp.

Three Wishes

Doris Lynch

"We don't like flowers that do not wilt; they must die…"
--Marianne Moore

If dying were only
a transformation from the ligature
of skin, muscle, and bone
into the wandering
evanescence of clouds

> But even rhinocerous-shaped clouds
> lose girth
> and fall back to earth.

When the minstrel of death approaches playing
his death flute, seize the list
he carelessly drops on your bed:
choose waterfall, willow & porcupine ways.

> Choose all three.
> Become a waterfall, a sashaying, wand-filled
> tree. Drape enlongated quills over a river,
> release into its quicksilver channel
> needles of wind-rippled glory.
> Watch them taunt fish to leap,
> bellow frogs to hush,

95

and order herons to jump
out of their skins toward the sky.

Miriam's Lantern

Ray Keifetz

"Under the spreading chestnut tree the village smithy stands."
                                                    --Longfellow

Chestnut trees really did shade the town where I learned to smith. My father apprenticed me after having read in some journal that the outlook for wagons and carriages had never been brighter. Henry Ford had just introduced the Model T, but that detail was overlooked by the journal. Also overlooked was what happened that afternoon in a nearby field.

That summer afternoon, while my father sat on the porch reading his journal, I went into the field with my two cousins and our three shotguns. We fired at whatever hopped, or fluttered, or cheeped – wrens, meadow larks, redwing blackbirds . . . I saw a bird I had never seen before, small, grey blue, and very round. I saw it in my sights. What a neat bird I thought and squeezed the trigger. I carried it home by its feet. My father putting down his journal said, Good shot, son. I didn't think there were any left.

Thus began my long apprenticeship. I learned to smelt and temper, cast and hammer, by the colors of fire – the ripe orange orange, the blinding yellow white, the deep ruby so like the eyes of that small dead bird. With every blow my arms grew stronger, the hammer lighter. Not only iron, my master said, we forge ourselves. So do we temper. Shoes by the hundreds, by the thousands, bits and bridles and

97

fittings – shackles I now know – but how beautiful and worthy I thought them then of the beasts they constrained. The shoeing – how fast could you take the flat stock and match it to a hoof. Our world rang with bells of bone and iron. Wooden wagons, carts and carriages, drawn by the great horses our hard hands had shod, streamed down the winding roads in an unstoppable flood. I was fast and strong, getting faster and stronger, and one afternoon I shouted, Bring on more work. I'm waiting –

I must have given offense. McAuliff the journeyman put down his hammer and crossed his arms. They were the width of chestnut limbs.

"What kind of fool are you, Marner, that you can't see?"

"I guess I can see as good as the next."

"Then why can't you see it ain't you that's gotten faster. It's the work that's gotten slower."

My route to work took me down an aisle of chestnut trees. These great trees shaded us in summer, fed us in the fall; their wood upon which dampness had scant effect timbered our barns and fenced our fields year round. My eagerness to reach the forge, the flames, turned my way into a green leafy blur. But a few days after offending the journeyman, I saw something that made me stop and stare. Maybe it was the falling leaves swirling sluggishly in the muggy air. Maybe it was the season – high summer and green everywhere – and that these leaves falling in clouds were dry and brown. I looked up. The entire crown was ablaze but without a single nut pod which would ripen and fall before the leaves. As I resumed my walk the far side of the trunk came into view. The rough bark was bloated with lumps and giant boils, split open with long vertical fissures dripping orange dust. I rushed from tree to tree, circled each trunk, looked up looked down . . . Some of them still appeared as if they might stand forever, but everywhere else the cracks, the boils, the orange dust . . .

When I reached the forge I said to McAuliff, "There's something happening to the trees!"

He said, "That is the least of your worries."

I stared at him and made another discovery. The journeyman's hair was gray. McAuliff had become an old man. Then I looked at the forge. Where were the flames? I threw on more wood, worked the bellows. The yellow flames leaped. Then I heard the Master calling my name and McAuliff saying better not to keep him waiting.

The Master was sitting behind his table – a log he'd split to test the edge of an axe and planed smooth. He was counting out some bills and coins. Without looking up he said, "Marner, I'm letting you go."

"After all these years – Without a hint – Without a warning – "

"Hint? Warning? Haven't you eyes?"

"It don't seem right.

"It ain't right," he said pushing the money towards me.

"All these years – " was what I said.

"You're still young," was what he answered.

It was the earliest autumn anyone could remember and for countless chestnut trees the last. They just flared up in a burst of brilliant color and died. The same also for many a forge and foundry. My first stop a group of men were sitting in front of a cold hearth, their arms enormous from when they still fed it.

"I'm looking for work."

"You find any, you let us know."

Before my eyes their great bare forearms began to swell and crack . . . I looked again and they were as before, dangling uselessly by their sides.

The road out of town was not the one I had come in on. Automobiles racing round the turns pushed me and the few remaining horse carts, drivers and horses choking into the brush. Almost a journeyman, I went from town to town climbing hills, dipping into hollows, searching for work. But everywhere the fires were dying. When I started my apprenticeship it was as though the stars in the sky for want of room had come down onto the hilltops and into the hollows between, so many stars twinkling up there and down here and now it seemed as if half the sky had been snuffed out. I walked through groves of dead chestnut trees, their limbs lying shattered at their feet. Here and there I'd come to a sapling shooting up pencil thin in a race against the blistering rust. One solitary fruit was now all they could bear, just enough to forward the agony. The blight had reduced the mighty trees to our condition: blooming and dying . . . rapidly.

Once in a long while I'd find a forge or foundry not yet snuffed and inquire after work. Experience? they'd ask and I would tell them proudly that I was almost a journeyman.

The first man said, and he more or less spoke for the few that followed, "I was kind of looking for someone without his way of doing so there'd be room to take in my way of doing."

"I can learn," I said.

"Not on my time."

Early winter followed early fall and spring was belated. I found work sharpening lawn mower blades and straightening bicycle frames. Puttering and sputtering at this and that I would hear as if he were standing right behind me my master's voice and I would repeat out loud his scornful words *you call yourself a smith,* pack up and move on.

Then I heard a rumor of a town deep in the woods which the blight had not yet reached, a town still needing a smith.

The town – Praywell – strange name – seemed in truth the answer to my prayers. Chestnut trees ripe with fruit, their trunks strong and sound, shaded a narrow street lined with the workshops of potters, spinners, weavers, glass blowers, turners and joiners . . . At the very end just before the street turned back into the woods stood an abandoned blacksmith shop, its forge gone out and cold. I told them I had no money, given even the shape the place was in, to buy it. They said you don't have to buy it, just light it and keep it lit, keep the forge burning. Here is all the flat stock you will need for shoes, iron enough to shoe a herd, rasps enough to bevel the world . . . But where, I asked, are my customers, my farmers and carriage makers –

"Gone," they said. "Surely you have seen . . ."

I said no more. For there were anvils and hammers and my arms were strong. There was a loft, warm and tight, and my body ached from the nights on the ground.

Thus resumed my long apprenticeship. Hour after hour I hammered out shoes no horse would ever wear and at the end of the day thrust them back into the flames, day after day starting anew what I had destroyed the night before. Separated by a sagging rope, I'd explain to the infrequent visitors down from the city to gape the colors of fire – the ripe orange orange, the blinding yellow white, the deep ruby so like the eyes of a small dead bird – explaining to the indifference beyond the rope what my life had been reduced to.

"So how does it feel to be a piece of living history?"

The last visitor had left hours ago and the shadows pressed against me. I turned and saw a woman standing at the rope, her face glowing in the forge light. Her hair was streaked with grey, she looked careworn but at the same time

101

almost young, youthful. There seemed to be two women facing me, an older graying one, and beneath a much younger one, and the fire was melting away the older and the younger was emerging from the flames –

"If you call it living," I said.

"I do," she said and wished me good night.

Every morning as I worked the bellows I'd watch for her walking past my open doors on the way to the meadow outside of town and I would watch for her return hours later, wicker baskets overflowing with roots and flowers. And all afternoon as I tended my own fire think of her, of Miriam tending her fires, her kettles boiling, her dyes spreading. In the evening when the last horseshoes had been melted flat, cooled and stacked, I would walk up and down Praywell's only street, my booted feet thumping the wooden planks, crickets singing in the trees. Back and forth from one end of town to the other I paced, passing the closed doors of joiners and weavers and spinners, passing the dyer's door, Miriam's. One evening as I approached her door for maybe the fourth time I saw that her light was still burning, a warm, inviting light that spilled through the cracks and formed a glowing pool at my feet. I knocked softly. Miriam opened and let me in.

"I'm working late," she said.

"But what is the point?" I said. "What we make goes nowhere."

"Nowhere?"

"I forge a hundred horseshoes only to melt them down again."

"And Matthew planes a hundred cherry wood boards. And planes them again. Lucy spins her thread from the skein she unraveled yesterday – "

"What futility!"

102

"Tell that to the nest building birds, to the spiders, the beavers, the ants . . . Tell that to the weavers and spinners and builders of the earth – "

"But those are animals."

"Yes," Miriam said. "They are."

Miriam continued stirring her dye. I peered into the kettle and saw our faces coming close together and the lantern above rippling back from the dark indigo. I said: "Sometimes it feels like a punishment."

She kept stirring and I kept peering. "A man apprentices himself for seven years, a man with arms like these, and he can't find a job. How can the world be so wide and have no room for a pair of skillful hands."

"There is room," she said. "Maybe not very much. Tucked away off to the side and in the far corners, you can still find some."

From then on I tried to work as if I had no mind, no aspirations, neither past nor future, as if the hammer, iron, and my arms were one, as if they had as much choice to rise and fall as my heart to beat. What is mastery anyway, Miriam had said, but a kind of forgetting. Day followed identical day, my speed increasing, my arms broadening. Whenever doubt darkened me I would glance in on Miriam. Her faith, her acceptance, was like a lantern whose light illuminated the vague outlines of a path which her smile invited me to follow.

As I was working the bellows one day, explaining the flames to a young couple behind the rope, I heard the young man whisper to the girl:

"It's like going to the zoo."

After they left I barred the doors and extinguished the forge. On the way out of town I stopped by Miriam's door to say goodbye.

"I can't stay here any longer."

"But why?"

"Look at my arms – " and I held them out to her. "Look how they've withered."

The world was wide after all. Why was I hiding like some criminal in a far corner? I went up to the city to try my luck. You can always find work in a city, particularly if you swallow your pride. Two blocks from the city zoo I found a room. I soon learned that it was in this very zoo, in the woods surrounding the caged animals, that the first blighted chestnut was discovered. At the earliest opportunity I paid a visit to see for myself the source of the contagion. That tree, however, had long since been felled: only its stump, wide enough to dance upon, remained ringed by sickly shoots. Though I had no further interest here, I nevertheless continued onwards, compelled it almost felt by someone or something calling to me in distress. Up ahead a group of boys were jeering at a curious, shaggy beast pacing back and forth in its cage. At my approach they moved on. The harmless seeming creature – singular, sterile, the sign said, its ferocious parents having been of different but closely related species – gave a soft growl and continued its interminable pacing. I wandered off the main road with its cages and pools and came to a brick building. There were no cages here. Instead a flock of fluttering leaflets pinned to a board offered employment opportunities. And as I had already passed the elephant house and seen the men going about with their shovels, I went in without reading further.

The man behind the desk looked as tired and faded as his brown suit. His name, Mr. Kearney, Irish I supposed. He asked me if I liked animals. I told him how before commencing my apprenticeship I had worked on a farm. He said I asked you if you liked animals. I miss the wagons, I said, the carriages. I miss them because of the horses and not just because I made my living from them, but for the sound of their hooves, the sparks flying . . .

"What about birds?

"I sure miss those horses."

"I'm asking you about birds."

"There used to be some. In the trees. There used to be some trees." Shaking his head, Mr. Kearney stood up and I did the same. After all there were plenty of other jobs in the city . . .

"You may work out," he said. "Because if you cared a jot, you wouldn't last an hour."

A chilling drizzle, typical of this city, had begun to fall. I followed Mr. Kearney past a line of shivering people.

"Some days there's nobody here," Mr. Kearney said. "Then some newspaperman happens to remember, writes a story . . ."

I glanced at the faces of the men and women – what were they hoping to find up ahead? – while Mr. Kearney went on about the fickleness of human beings, how they never seemed to care about anything until the situation was past caring, as for instance the passing of beings other than themselves by which I understood him to mean animals, but of whom he spoke with reverence as if their presence or absence among us were on a par with heaven and our future therein. From these remarks, and from the hundreds of people waiting patiently in the miserable weather, I concluded that something huge and splendid must be dying.

At a nod from Mr. Kearney a uniformed guard announced that the building was closed and that all were welcome to return tomorrow. We had it to ourselves, the dark, deserted interior in which a lone cylindrical mesh cage illuminated by a single spotlight's downward beam occupied the center.

"Take a good look, Marner. In my lifetime their migrations darkened the sky. Take a good look. For now and forever you're looking at the last of them."

Even before he spoke I had already recognized the small bluish bird against whose eyes I gauged my fires –

"There were millions of them once," he said. "As recent as fifteen years ago so called sportsmen were still organizing shoots – As recent as ten years ago," he said, "boys with guns were popping them out of trees. I ask you, Marner, can such people be forgiven?"

The bird swiveled its head and fixed me with its blood red eye.

"No," I whispered. "And they should not be."

We stayed in that dark room for hours staring and breathing. I felt Mr. Kearney beside me, his outrage, his pity. I felt, as with myself, that he could not remove his eyes from the small bird perched alone on a dowel. I kept waiting for Mr. Kearney to raise his voice, to shout down the shotgun blasts reverberating through the aviary, but he must have been waiting for me to do the same.

"What do you want of me?" I said.

"It's very simple," he answered. "I want you to watch."

I was issued a uniform and instructed to keep back the crowds, though a slack rope suspended between opposite walls would have sufficed. Most of the time there were no crowds, only a hungry, waiting silence which I tried to keep back as well. Day after day I watched the bird whose solitude could not be measured. The passing of an entire race, Mr. Kearney said, must not go unnoticed. Can't you see the multitudes, the whirling dark clouds, the endless blue light, the generations fluttering and breathing because this lone individual continues to breath and flutter? I saw only a small solitary bird, a small solitary ending, which took red berries from my hand. Its bluish head swiveling iridescently from side to side, what did it see? Day and night I brooded on letting the bird go. Together the two of us of unrelated but

106

closely connected species, from separate but closely related cages would rise up into the sky –

Not a day passed without Mr. Kearney looking in.

"When nothing else is left," he said, "there's the waiting."

The bird sidled down its dowel towards Mr. Kearney.

"It knows you," I said.

"These birds mate for life. They're not meant to be alone."

"Maybe another will turn up."

"The last one turned up about nine years ago on a kitchen pile – a few bones, a few feathers, a lot of buckshot."

"Maybe in some far off spot – "

"Where?"

"Some tucked away spot," I said, "where the boys don't carry guns." And I started to cough.

The cough got worse, my breath rattled through the darkness, but the nature of my work forbade me to miss a single day. Even on my days off you would find me leaning over the guard rail, eyes fixed on the tiny bird perched behind the mesh. I asked Mr. Kearney how old did he guess the bird to be, what age did he expect the bird to reach. It was hard to say, Mr. Kearney said. It seemed a healthy specimen.

And yet I sensed that beneath its soft plush plumage, as with me beneath my sweat stiff uniform, the plump little bird was slowly withering. Slowly, irrevocably, but with a hearty appetite. Day after day I fed it the red berries that he loved and watched. I watched and waited, my ragged breath filling the dark room. And the tiny bird gazed back at me and at whomever else was there or not there, at all of us, the present and absent with equal equanimity, as if presence or absence beyond the mesh could not have the slightest impact on the greater absence within. Every morning covered in sweat from a night of not sleeping, I would rush from my room to the wire mesh whose sign in the language of verdicts

107

declared *No others are known* – lest that verdict be commuted in my absence to *None* . . . I lost all sense of days, months, years, the difference between, between a day and a year, a moment and a lifetime; there were only days now, only one day really – And then I woke to a strange stillness. The shotguns had ceased their blasting. I seemed to see my face as if reflected in a deep well and beside my face, almost touching, the dyer Miriam's – and from these signs I understood that *the day* had come. Wheezing, scarcely able to breathe, I rushed to the cage. But there it sat as usual upon its dowel thin perch, unchanged, unchanging, swiveling its head in my direction as I pitched forward towards its feet.

It was Mr. Kearney who found me at the foot of the cage, my fingers wrapped around a handful of red berries, and shook me awake. For a moment the two of us crouched there together on the cold cement floor, the light from above, a light so familiar, so soothing, cascading down on us, bathing us in radiance. I lifted my eyes and for an instant beheld in this glimmering true light not only the one last bird but all the birds, the multitudes in swirling flight, the nest builders, weavers . . . other creatures as well, the diggers, burrowers, the builders of this earth who do their work without cease or complaint. Mr. Kearney helped me to my feet, but it was not only Mr. Kearney. The cage was brilliantly illuminated and the little bird clearly perched within, yet flapping its short stubby wings he seemed to be helping me up too as if somehow he had managed to enter my cage or I had fallen into his.

"I was wrong about you, Marner," Mr. Kearney said. "You do care."

"I was hoping I would die first. I was trying . . ."

Soon after, Mr. Kearney let me go. It was a kindness.

I packed a rucksack with food – bagfuls of red berries and for myself dry bread, hard cheese – and set out for the hills and hollows, the woods and open fields of my childhood. The countryside had become even darker as if somewhere the dikes and sandbags had all collapsed, and I made my way as through a dark flood. Yet my heart was buoyant, for perhaps this darkness had to be if I were to pick out the faint glimmering, the unassuming radiance of Miriam's lantern and by its light take up again, for now and forever, my unfinished apprenticeship.

One Arm Might Reach the Ocean

Mabel Yu

I shivered. Maybe, it was cold that night
and my skin drank the dampness
of his brick basement room.

I don't remember that, or how he felt
beside me, or how we'd felt
together, bodies rubbing like erasers,
trying to fix mistakes. I can't see
my wild hair or his sloped back, but I see
a browned apple core in an ash tray,
and a red tin alarm clock with eager bells,
like ears, on its ticking face. I remember

our desperation, how hard we'd grabbed each other
the way people do before saying goodbye. Mostly,
I remember the train rattling down a bridge nearby,
encompassing us in the hum of heavy wheels. Feeling
rolled over, sealed into a rundown tomb, I thought
of stacked cargo heading somewhere I hadn't been—
Indiana, Ohio, somewhere with fields of green
corn shaking the winter from their ears. A boxcar
full of bicycles with high shine silver spokes, another
with bolts of fabric: lightning spikes, checkers and tiny
pea flowers dotting calico and quilting to be snipped

and stitched to fit bodies and beds warmer
than mine. I wanted to be on those boxcars,
balancing their rumbling bodies tightly, so close
to tipping over, so adamant about running away.

The International Trade City, Yiwu

Mabel Yu

Every product is available in every color here: tiny gold
Buddhas, pink water guns, green inflatable fish, purple silk
flowers. They bargain in English and cheat you in Chinese.
They haggle while giant paintings of the Virgin Mary frame
their heads, or argue in stalls with rubber flip flops packing
the walls, stifling the air with the smell of tires. The nearby
factories turn out tired workers and bins of bra hooks or
crates of Halloween masks. The employees do not know
what Halloween is and cannot imagine the impetus to put a
turtle's face on theirs, or a superman, or a ghost.

At night, they break from dormitories to watch kung fu
movies in the streets from a white screen tied, like a kite, to a
cargo truck. The kids squat, transfixed, or try kicks on the
outskirts of the crowd. Adults sing karaoke under white and
blue lights. They pack, and seal, and do not notice anymore
the stamps or stickers of Made in China. They will sell you
anything you want. They built their city on the belief that you
want, and want is a colored thing in red and yellow and gold.

Contributors

William Archila lives in Los Angeles, California, with his wife. His poems have been published in *The Georgia Review*, *AGNI*, *Poetry International*, *The Los Angeles Review*, *Notre Dame Review*, *Crab Orchard Review*, *Obsidian III*, *Rattle*, and *Blue Mesa Review*, among others. His poems also will be appearing in *Poet Lore* and *Cold Mountain Review*. His first book is *The Art of Exile* (Bilingual Press, 2009).

Nicole Ausmus has been creating prose since she was able to put pen to paper. As a busy mother of two lovely, creative daughters, finding time to write can be difficult, but subject material is never an issue. Married to her best friend, Nicole has received invaluable encouragement in her endeavor to become a noted poet and novelist. Her passion for writing has been heavily influenced by her mother, Candace Mulligan, who had short fiction published in *Paper Radio* and *Tin Roof*, and was a regular guest reader at *Powell's Bookstores* and *Common Grounds*. Nicole's current projects include grant writing, a memoir, an anthology of poetry, and a cookbook for busy parents.

Danielle Bauman is a native New Yorker with a BFA in acting from Boston University. She is an actor, director, and writer of plays, prose, and poetry. Her poem "My Ex Boyfriend was a Pair of Shoes" appears in *Locust Magazine*. She lives in Brooklyn with her incredibly supportive family and inspirational cat Mimi.

Patrick Carrington is the author of *Hard Blessings* (MSR Publishing, 2008), *Thirst* (Codhill, 2007), and *Rise, Fall and Acceptance* (MSR Publishing, 2006), and winner of *New Delta Review's* Matt Clark Prize and *Yemassee's* Pocataligo Contest in poetry. His poems are forthcoming in *The American Poetry*

Journal, Notre Dame Review, The National Poetry Review, The Connecticut Review, and elsewhere. He teaches creative writing in New Jersey and serves as the poetry editor of *Mannequin Envy* (www.mannequinenvy.com).

Meagan Cass's fiction has appeared in *Carve Magazine, The South Carolina Review,* and in the *Minnetonka Review,* where it received the 2007 Editor's Prize. She earned her BA at Binghamton University and her MFA at Sarah Lawrence College. She is currently a Ph.D. candidate in English at the University of Louisiana Lafayette, where she teaches Creative Writing and American Literature, and edits *Rougarou,* the department's online, national literary journal.

Lisa Fay Coutley is an MFA candidate at Northern Michigan University, where she teaches writing and serves as an Assistant Poetry Editor for *Passages North.* She also holds an MA in creative nonfiction. Her poetry has appeared, or is forthcoming, in *The Pedestal Magazine, The Brooklyn Review, Eclipse, Terminus,* and others.

Patrick Michael Finn's first book, the novella *A Martyr for Suzy Kosasovich,* was selected by Tom Barbash as winner of the 2006 Ruthanne Wiley Memorial Novella Competition and published by The Cleveland State University Poetry Center. A winner of the AWP Intro Award, selected by Benjamin Alire Sáenz, and the 2004 Third Coast Fiction Prize, judged by Stuart Dybek, Finn's stories have appeared or are forthcoming in *Ploughshares, TriQuarterly, Third Coast, Quarterly West, Punk Planet, The Yalobusha Review,* and Houghton Mifflin's *The Best American Mystery Stories 2004.* His fiction has also received citations in the *2005 Pushcart Prize* and *The Best American Short Stories 2008.* Finn's second book, a collection of stories titled *From the Darkness Right Under Our Feet,* won the

2009 Hudson Prize and is forthcoming from Black Lawrence Press, an imprint of Dzanc Books, in 2011.

Laurie Frankel's fiction and creative nonfiction have appeared in *The Pedestal Magazine*, *Under the Sun*, *Green Mountains Review* and she was twice a finalist for *Glimmer Train's Very Short Fiction Award*. Her book, *It's Not Me, It's You* has been translated and is now in its third printing. Contact her at LauriesLoveLogic.com.

Rodney Gomez lives in Brownsville, Texas, and is a student in the new MFA in Creative Writing program at the University of Texas – Pan American. Recently, he was a resident at the Atlantic Center for the Arts and his poems appear in *Denver Quarterly*, *Barrow Street*, *The Literary Review*, *The Pinch*, and *Hawai'i Review*.

Arthur Gottlieb is an Oregon poet whose work has appeared in many small literary magazines, including *The Ledge*, *Chiron Review*, *The Alembic*, *The Pacific Review*, and *Lullwater Review*.

Loren Graham has taught creative writing at Lynchburg College, James Madison University, and Hollins University. He currently teaches at Carroll College in Helena, Montana. His first book of poetry, *Mose*, was published by Wesleyan University Press in 1994. His new collection of sonnets and anti-sonnets is entitled *The Ring Scar* (Word Press, 2010).

Jenny Hanning lives in Austin, Texas. Her fiction and poetry have appeared in *Shenandoah*, *Post Road*, *Quarterly West*, and others.

Rick Henry has published fiction and articles in a variety of journals and anthologies, most recently *Chant: A Romance* (BlazeVox Books, 2008) and *Lucy's Eggs and Other Stories*

(Syracuse UP, 2006). His other books include: *Pretending and Meaning: Toward a Pragmatic Theory of Fictional Discourse*, a philosophical inquiry (Greenwood Publishing, 1996); and *Sidewalk Portrait: Fifty-fourth Floor and Falling*, a novella (BlazeVox Books, 2006). In addition, he is co-editor of *The Blueline Anthology* (Syracuse UP, 2004).

H. L. Hix's most recent poetry collection is *Legible Heavens* (Etruscan Press, 2008). He teaches at the University of Wyoming.

Ray Keifetz lives in Northern California, where he earns his living selling wine and building furniture. His stories and poems have appeared recently in *The Iodine Poetry Journal*, *The Dos Passos Review*, and *Skidrow Penthouse*. Previous publications include *Other Voices* and *The North Atlantic Review*. He is nearing completion of a collection of stories whose common theme may be gleaned from the title: *The Hidden Cost of Gifts*.

Mark Liebenow grew up in Wisconsin hiking through the woods. He moved to California and hiked along the Pacific Ocean. He now lives in Illinois where he hikes through cornfields. Besides poetry, he writes about Yosemite and recovery from grief. He has also written about the theology of clowning and teaching living skills to the mentally challenged.

Ann Linde's chapbook, *Courting Light*, was published by Finishing Line Press. She received her MFA in poetry from the University of Minnesota. Her awards include a residency at the Anderson Center for Interdisciplinary Studies and an Academy of American Poets James Wright Prize. She works as an English instructor.

116

Janet Lyn lives in Portland, Oregon, works for Ashford University, and mothers five children. She supports Iris Ministries Inc, Born2Fly International, and Pure Desire Ministries International. When she has spare change, she enjoys fried bananas with coconut ice cream and raspberry sauce at The Frog Thai Cuisine on McLoughlin Blvd.

Doris Lynch recently published poetry in *The Innisfree Poetry Journal, The Adirondack Review, The Tipton Poetry Review, Xanadu,* and *Commonweal.* The Indiana Arts Commission has awarded her three individual artist's grants. She works as an adult services librarian and loves hiking in the West, particularly in New Mexico and Alaska, where she previously lived.

Joe Pitkin lives in Vancouver, WA, where he teaches English at Clark College. His work has appeared previously in *North American Review, Beloit Poetry Journal, The Portland Review,* and elsewhere.

Dave Seter was born in Chicago. He studied creative writing at Princeton University, where he earned his degree in civil engineering. He continues to practice engineering in the San Francisco Bay Area. His poems have appeared in various journals, including *Karamu, California Quarterly, Kerf, Blue Collar Review, Raven Chronicles,* and *Switched-On Gutenberg.* His chapbook *Night Duty* was published by Main Street Rag in 2010.

Harding Stedler was named the first Professor Emeritus at Shawnee State University in Ohio at the time of his retirement. In retirement, he makes his home in Arkansas where he is a member of the River Market Poets, the Lucidity Poets, and the Poets' Roundtable of Arkansas. He has recently founded the Frontier Poets in his hometown of Maumelle.

Laura Swindlehurst of Seattle is a freelance writer and recent graduate of the University of Washington. Her short story "Notes" is her first published work of fiction. She is currently working on a short story collection inspired by her experiences living in the Pacific Northwest.

Over eighty poems of **Ann Tweedy**'s poems have been published in journals and anthologies, including *Gertrude*, *Rattle*, *Damselfly Press*, and *Clackamas Literary Review*, and she has been nominated for a Pushcart Prize. Her chapbook *Beleaguered Oases* is forthcoming from TcCreativePress in Los Angeles, and individual poems are forthcoming in *Martin Luther King, Jr.: A Multicultural Anthology* and *Meditations on Divine Names: An Anthology of Contemporary Poetry*. Her manuscripts have also been selected as finalists for the Bluelight Press Annual Chapbook Competition, the Robin Becker Chapbook Contest, and the New Sins Press Poetry Book Award, among others. Originally from Massachusetts, she currently divides her time between Skagit County, Washington, and San Diego. You can read more of her poetry at www.anntweedypoetry.com.

Wendy Willis is a mother, lawyer, knitter, gardener, and poet who lives in Portland, Oregon, with her two young daughters. She is the Deputy Director for National Programs at the National Policy Consensus Center at Portland State University. She has had poems published in a variety of national and regional journals.

Mabel Yu was born and raised in the Washington, DC, Metro Area. She received her MFA from Eastern Washington

University. Her work has appeared in *Knockout* and is forthcoming in *Quarter After Eight* and *Inkwell*.